DESERT DREAMWEAVER

Katie goes on impulse for a few weeks . . . Alysha goes hoping to find her roots . . . Amongst the stony wastes of the Northern Cape in South Africa both girls find excitement and intrigue. They help a group of workers who are drilling for water and starting a school for a local tribe — an activity that turns out to be more interesting and fulfilling than they'd ever imagined. And while they are working, one of the girls finds romance . . .

Books by Ginny Swart
in the Linford Romance Library:

HEART OF AFRICA
CAMPAIGN FOR LOVE
UNDER THE AFRICAN SUN

GINNY SWART

DESERT DREAMWEAVER

Complete and Unabridged

LINFORD
Leicester

First published in Great Britain in 2010

First Linford Edition
published 2011

British Library CIP Data

Swart, Ginny.
  Desert dreamweaver. - -
  (Linford romance library)
  1. Voluntarism- -South Africa- -Northern
  Cape- -Fiction. 2. Love stories.
  3. Large type books.
  I. Title II. Series
  823.9′2–dc22

  ISBN 978–1–4448–0742–4

Published by
F. A. Thorpe (Publishing)
Anstey, Leicestershire

Set by Words & Graphics Ltd.
Anstey, Leicestershire
Printed and bound in Great Britain by
T. J. International Ltd., Padstow, Cornwall

This book is printed on acid-free paper

Compliment

Katie Norris opened the beautiful white wedding album with the embossed silver bells on the cover, and looked at the empty first page.

Which photograph to paste first? A brand-new album was always an exciting prospect. She felt the thrill of anticipation, like an artist with a blank canvas, with a brush full of paint ready to create a masterpiece.

Only this masterpiece would be a book full of precious memories for the McGillivray couple.

Should she use the one of Morag standing alone next to the oak tree before she left for the church, or the one of Morag and Jim together? They were arm-in-arm on the steps of St Michael's after the ceremony, sprinkled with rose petals and looking so happy.

She had almost decided on the one of

1

Morag alone, with the sunlight behind her giving her beautiful white beaded dress a luminous quality, when her eyes were suddenly covered by a pair of strong hands.

'Connor Bradfield!' she spluttered. 'Don't do that!'

'How did you know it was me, then?' Connor asked, kissing her cheek and settling his lanky form down on the chair next to her.

'Because I don't know anyone else daft enough to come creeping up behind me and frighten the life out of me.' She grinned. 'Well, seeing as you're here, which picture do you think should be on the front page of the album?'

'Ah, the McGillivrays' wedding?' Connor took both pictures and studied them critically.

'They're both terrific. But I'd say the one of both of them together. You've really caught that magic moment there.'

'Do you think so?' Katie asked, pleased by the compliment. 'Right.'

Connor looked through the others

while she worked.

'This is, what, your twentieth wedding?' he asked. 'You're getting a name as a wedding photographer, you know. I heard them in the village saying nice things about you. 'The lassie from London always takes a bonnie picture.''

'You're just saying that because you want an invitation to supper,' she teased. 'You should rather butter up my mum. She's the one in charge of the kitchen, once she gets back from the town.'

Proud

'Hello, you two. Did I hear my name mentioned?'

Helen Norris breezed into the room, followed by two dogs and the farm cat.

'Hi, Mrs Norris. Let me help you with those.'

Connor leaped up and took the shopping bags from Katie's mother and carried them through to the kitchen, almost bumping his head on the lintel of the door. Old farmhouses were not designed for men of six-foot-three.

Helen Norris smiled at him.

'Thanks, Connor. You're a dear. You wouldn't like to stay for a bite to eat, by any chance?'

She and Katie exchanged amused glances and they both burst out laughing. Connor's fondness for Helen's cooking was legendary. Ever since he and Katie had started going out together six months before, he'd been a regular visitor round about teatime.

'Well, if you're sure . . . If you've enough . . . '

'There's always enough for one more, Connor. Especially for a man who's not shy about washing up afterwards.'

'Ah, you know me, Mrs Norris, I love washing dishes!'

'Your mum really brought you up well, lad.'

She had, too, Katie thought fondly, gazing at Connor as he helped her mother pack away the groceries. He was a real gentleman, the sort of man who opened doors for girls and stood up when older people entered the room.

In fact, that was how Katie had met him.

He'd stood aside for her and opened the door to the butcher's shop when she was going in to collect the weekly order for her mother, and she'd tripped over his size twelve feet.

She would have gone flying if he

hadn't let go of the door and caught her, and as she'd looked up at him and caught the twinkle in his eyes, she'd thought, well, at least there is one nice man here in Strathcorn!

He'd insisted on taking her for a cup of tea next door to make sure she was all right and things had slowly progressed from there.

Of course, Strathcorn was a small town and that evening, when Katie mentioned how she'd met Connor, it turned out her mother knew far more about him than she did.

'Betty Bradfield's a member of our book club,' she said. 'She's so proud of Connor. He's her only son. He was very clever, you know; won all the prizes at school and got a good scholarship to college down south somewhere. Now he's a qualified accountant and he could have taken a job anywhere — London, Edinburgh, even overseas — but he chose to come back home and work.

'A very good lad. And I believe he just bought his own house in Myrtle

Avenue. He's doing very well.'

Even before she met him, it was clear that Mrs Norris thoroughly approved. Connor spent five days of the week wearing a suit as a junior accountant with the firm of Swigg Brothers in town. But at the weekends he liked nothing better than helping Katie's father with the cows, mucking in almost like one of the family. In six short months he'd almost become the son they never had and Katie knew that they hoped she and Connor were serious.

But she wasn't ready to get serious with anyone. She needed her own space once again, a place she could decorate and furnish as she wanted. It was very comfortable, moving back to her old room in the house where she was born, but it was definitely time to move on.

★   ★   ★

Listening to her mother and Connor chatting in the kitchen like old friends

7

while Connor sliced the onions for chicken curry, she realised it was time she announced her plans.

'I've found a little flat in town,' she said loudly. 'Above the stationer's in the high street. I'm signing the lease next week.'

Her mother stopped putting away the sugar and came through to the dining-room.

'But, darling, I didn't think you were serious when you talked of finding your own flat! I thought you were so happy here. You know Dad and I love having you back with us. There's plenty of room . . . '

'I know, Mum. It's been great living at home again but I need my own place,' she said, giving her mother a hug.

'A flat of your own sounds good,' Connor said. 'But signing a lease? For how long?'

'A year, to start with.'

'But maybe you shouldn't tie yourself down for a whole year,' he protested.

'You wouldn't be free to move any-where. Or go anywhere exciting.'

'I don't want to move. I'm quite happy back in Strathcorn. Not that I ever thought I'd say that, but I am.'

Memories

Katie fell silent, remembering her five years as a professional photographer for a big advertising agency in London. From this distance, her time there seemed like a dream, something that had happened to someone else.

At first, she'd thought her life was almost perfect. She'd worked with two others in a studio equipped with the latest and most expensive cameras and her daily work gave her a variety of challenging subjects.

The studio artists demanded something different, something edgy and off the wall, which suited Katie's style of photography beautifully. In her second year with Matheson's she'd been promoted to studio manager.

'You're a bit young for the job but you've got an eye for exactly what we're looking for,' Joe, the director, said.

'That campaign you did to promote awareness for the homeless was a real winner. But this promotion means longer hours and overall responsibility for the studio. Do you think you're up to it?'

'Of course I am,' she said, glowing.

She won praise from clients as well as the others in the agency and her professional life had been satisfying and successful

And sharing a flat with the glamorous PR of the agency had been a lot of fun.

Alysha Mabenda was a stunningly beautiful dark-skinned girl with a wicked sense of humour and a loud belly-laugh that made everyone who heard it smile.

The girls' social life had been filled with noisy evenings at the smartest clubs in town and weekends away for parties and dances. Some days Katie went to work after only a few hours' sleep and kept going on cups of black coffee and the adrenaline of an urgent deadline to meet.

And for a year or two there was Allan, a computer programmer whom she'd met at a party and who had become an important part of her life. For a while she'd been sure they'd marry one day, when Allan felt ready to settle down.

But last year they'd started drifting apart and had finally broken up by mutual agreement. He'd gone off to work in Australia and she'd waved him farewell with no regrets. But her life felt surprisingly empty after he left, even though the round of parties and clubbing continued.

Last year her frantically busy, fun-filled life in the city had started to pall. Every day, the work in the studio began to feel the same and she no longer looked forward to her job as studio manager. The sparkle had gone.

By December she was exhausted and really needed the week's break back on the farm.

Seven wonderful, cold, crisp days, meeting old friends and a round of visits to her extended family made it very difficult to go back to London and, although she returned feeling recharged, she wasn't really looking forward to the new year ahead.

Suddenly everything about London seemed too noisy and dirty and rushed. Katie couldn't get used to the traffic and the endless waiting for the Tube and the crowds on the pavements. Life in the big city had lost its attraction and some days it felt as though the walls of the stuffy, airless studio were closing in on her.

Decision

'I need a change,' she said to Alysha soon after her holiday. 'Another job. Maybe I should go freelance so I'd get out and about more. The thought of that studio tomorrow just fills me with gloom.'

'You've stayed too long in the wilds of Scotland, that's your trouble,' Alysha said flippantly. 'Come on, the guys said they'd meet us at the club tonight. You'd better get dressed.'

'Count me out,' Katie said shortly. 'I just don't feel like all that loud music. I think I'll just stay at home with a good book.'

'Are you sick, girl?' Half joking, Alysha felt her forehead. 'Friday night is not a night for a good book!'

Katie grinned.

'I'm fine. I just feel like taking it easy, that's all. You go on your own and tell me about it tomorrow.' Although, to tell the truth, she was feeling unusually tired. That night, as she lay in bed, she started to plan how she'd hand in her notice. I'll tell Joe that I'll continue until March, she thought. That'll give him time to find my replacement.

She tried to imagine how he'd react when she told him that she was leaving. Would he try to persuade her to stay by offering her a pay rise? But it wasn't about money. And where would she go when she resigned? Somewhere smaller than London, that was for sure. And what would she do? She didn't know, but she was certain of one thing — she needed a change of scene.

Then as she turned off the light, her chest began to tighten and she suddenly started to wheeze. In a rush, she remembered her old childhood battle with asthma, something she thought she'd completely outgrown years ago.

The wheezing didn't last long but it left her shaken and anxious, and the next morning she felt tired and weak. If it happened again she'd definitely see the doctor.

A week later she had another attack, more severe this time, while Alysha was in the flat.

Alysha looked anxiously at her flat-mate.

'Katie, that breathing sounds terrible. You're going to see the doctor this afternoon, no arguments.'

She hadn't the energy to protest and meekly thanked Alysha when she told her that she'd made an appointment for three o'clock.

Katie was pretty sure the doctor would just suggest carrying around one of those nifty little inhalers to use when necessary, but to her surprise he gave her a thorough once over, asked her about her daily life and ordered X-rays.

'There's nothing the matter with your lungs,' he finally said. 'But I think you're pretty run down. I'm going to recommend an iron tonic. But these asthma attacks are a worry. They could be brought on by stress, or pollution, or a combination of both. Whatever it is, you need a complete change, young lady. Tell me, where are you from, originally?'

'My parents have a dairy farm in Scotland, near a little town called Strathcorn, and I lived there until I went away to college in Elgin. Then five years ago I came down here to London.'

'Hmm,' he said. 'And what sort of job do you do now?'

'I'm head of the photographic studio at Matheson Advertising.'

'Aha.' He looked at her quizzically. 'Chemicals up your nose and down your air passages. Deadlines to meet and a daily dose of stress, am I right?'

'Yes,' she admitted softly.

'Well, to start with, you need to get away from any sort of air pollution,' he continued firmly. 'I'd really like to pack you off to a desert with nothing but hot, dry air, but seeing as that's not possible, living in the country as far away from the chemical soup you're breathing in in this city would be best for you.'

'But what about my job?' she protested weakly.

'You need to take care of yourself and nothing is more important than your health. Give yourself a year in the countryside with clean air, away from stress of any sort, and we'll talk again, all right?'

★ ★ ★

Katie had walked back to the flat, shocked. She had expected some sort of medication or treatment, not banishment from the life she'd known for five years!

But a small voice inside her rejoiced. Now she wouldn't have to explain to the director that she was just tired of the work and felt like moving on. She was under doctor's orders and he couldn't argue with that.

So there were no difficult decisions to make. She'd been told to go back to

Strathcorn, to the peace and quiet she'd so enjoyed during her holiday, and that was exactly what she would do, while she planned her next move.

And as for what that would be — well, she had an excellent camera, and the awards hanging on the studio wall told her she was a good photographer. She could take photographs for a living wherever she was.

I'll be free! She did a little skip at the thought of it and smiled at the man waiting for a bus. No more waiting for the Tube and standing all the way to work.

I'll miss Alysha, though, she thought. I just hope she won't be too upset now that she'll have to find someone else to share the rent.

Surprise

When Katie opened the door of the flat, a loud drumbeat rhythm was pounding out and Alysha floated into the front room wearing one of her colourful kente cloth kaftans, her long hair pinned up underneath an elaborate turban. She was grinning widely.

'Katie, my darlin'! You will never guess! My life is about to change! I have been *head hunted*!'

Alysha grabbed Katie by the hands and waltzed her round the tiny sitting-room. Her news was far too important not to be told and she didn't notice that Katie was unusually quiet.

'Remember that fellow from Dream-works Modelling who came into the office last week?'

'Vaguely.'

'Desmond Ford. Well, he just happened to invite me to lunch today. And he just happened to ask if he could take some shots of me, and guess what? He says the camera loves me! He's offered me a job and I'm going to be a model! Goodbye, Matheson's, hello big time! I'm off to Bermuda!'

'Wow.' Katie sat down, stunned. 'I don't know what to say. That's fantastic.'

'Yes, isn't it? Desmond's flying three of us — me and two others — down there for a beach shoot. We get to stay in some fabulous hotel right on the water and wear gorgeous clothes and do nothing except smile at the camera!'

'What did Joe say about your leaving?'

'He understood. I mean, he was a bit annoyed but Desmond phoned him and persuaded him to let me go. So there are no hard feelings. And I'll be earning loads of money. It's unbelievable what they pay models!'

'And you're leaving tomorrow?'

'Yep. I'd better start packing. Hey, have we any champagne in the fridge?

We should celebrate!'

Katie's news seemed pretty ordinary compared with Alysha's. Telling her she was resigning from her job because she needed a change sounded awfully hollow compared with jetting off to Bermuda.

But after the second glass of bubbly she plucked up the courage.

'I'm handing in my notice, too. The doctor says the London pollution's not good for my lungs and this asthma is caused by all the stress. So I've got to leave the studio and go home to my folks and — and milk the cows!'

Thanks to the champagne, this sounded terribly funny and both girls burst into uproarious laughter.

'You — milk the cows! Woo!' Alysha spluttered. 'I can just see that. My friend Katie, the cowgirl!'

'My dad uses milking machines,' Katie said, grinning. 'But I'll find something to do up there. Something to do with photography. Maybe get a job on the local newspaper. Whatever it is, it's going to be a whole new life. Actually, I can't wait.'

'A new life for us both,' Alysha said softly. 'But we mustn't lose touch, OK?'

'Of course we won't,' Katie said. 'Send me a postcard from all those exotic places you're going to be visiting and I'll send you one of some cows.'

'It's a deal,' Alysha said. 'We'll always keep in touch.'

Job-hunting

Her parents had been delighted to have her home again, although at first her mother hovered over her anxiously.

'It's lovely to have you home for a good long holiday, darling. Aren't we lucky! There's so much you can do to help out, when you're feeling up to it, that is.'

'Mum, I'm not feeling sick! In fact, I've had no trouble since I arrived. Please stop fussing. And I don't mind helping out here at all, but I want to find some proper work as soon as possible.'

'Well, I've started selling veggie seedlings at the farmers' market, did I tell you? You could help me pricking those out. It's easy and absolutely no stress!'

'Mum, I'm going to find something to do in my own line. Photography. I can't just stop working.'

'But the stress — the doctor said it

24

wasn't good for you.'

Katie looked out of the window at the herd of her father's cows beyond the fence, chewing rhythmically.

'Does this look like a stressful scene? Stress is waking in the middle of the night, remembering something you have to do the next day and not being able to go to sleep again, and when you walk into the studio you have two telephones ringing at the same time, your assistant calling in sick and just as the model who is costing five hundred pounds an hour arrives, the shutter of your camera jams and . . . '

'All right, so there's no stress here!' Mrs Norris laughed. 'Remember that old photo shop on the high street? Why not pop in and see him some time; maybe Mr Scott needs an assistant.'

★   ★   ★

Katie went into town the very next day. She enjoyed walking down the high street, so familiar to her from her

25

schooldays. Nothing had changed — the butcher and the newsagent still looked the same, and Madame Louise, the dress shop, still decorated its window with one solitary dress. She'd been told that a glitzy shopping mall had opened on the outskirts but she decided she'd support the older businesses in the town for as long as she could.

The photo shop, called Snappit, consisted of a small room with a counter and a selection of spools past their sell-by date in a basket next to an old-fashioned till.

The walls were decorated with faded photographs of family groups smiling stiffly for the camera and an out-of-date notice about an outing for the Camera Club. It didn't look very promising.

Happy To Help

At first the room appeared to be empty and she was about to ping the bell on the counter when Mr Scott suddenly emerged from underneath.

'Ah! Just looking for some invoices on the bottom shelf. I'm sure I put them in a box but I can't seem to find them . . . Yes! Good morning. What can I do for you, my dear?'

'I was wondering if you needed an assistant? I'm a photographer.'

Even as she said this she knew what his answer would be.

'You're a photographer, eh? So am I. And let me tell you, young lady, this town doesn't need one photographer, let alone two. I'm closing at the end of this month.'

'Oh.'

'It's all this digital stuff. People take their own pictures these days. I used to specialise in family groups, as you can see.' He waved his hand at the gallery around him. 'But no-one's interested nowadays. They don't care about good lighting or tastefully arranged groups or soft-focus shots. All they want is casual snaps. Any monkey can take those, it's all too easy.

'No, I'm packing up after thirty years in business here. Going down to Cornwall to live with my son.'

'I'm sorry to hear that,' Katie said sincerely, her heart sinking. If there wasn't enough work to keep Mr Scott busy, how could she expect to find any?

She'd try the 'Strathcorn Courier'. She'd noticed the newspaper offices around the corner and maybe they could use a freelance photographer.

The 'Courier' staff consisted of one girl and Billy Sharp, the editor.

'Photographer from London, eh?' Billy grinned at her across his desk. 'Bit of a comedown, working back here, isn't it?'

'Not at all,' she said stoutly. 'I wanted

28

to come back. And I'm hoping you'll have something I could do, as a sort of roving photographer, if you don't employ one full-time.'

'We only go to press once a week, on a Friday,' Billy said. 'And we've never needed a full-time photographer because my wife takes any pictures that are required. Council events, flower shows, that sort of thing. Gives her a bit of pin money.

'Otherwise, people send in their own pictures and if they're clear enough, we're happy to use them. Like this one.' He picked up a photograph of a small girl standing next to a Dalmatian. 'Winner of the dog show. Nice shot. We'll be using that on the front page this week.'

'The *front page*?'

'Well, the dog belongs to old man Weatherly.'

Katie looked at him blankly.

'Weatherly's Fine Foods. They're one of our biggest advertisers and this kid is his granddaughter. I know he'll appreciate the gesture. Can't go wrong with kids and dogs, you know.'

Katie smiled ruefully.

'Well, if your wife is ever unable to take the shot for any reason, give me a call. I'd be happy to help out.'

An Invitation

She drove home gloomily. 'I might have to look for something over in Glen Tarry,' she told her mother over lunch. 'I'll go next week.'

But the following day she met Connor, and over their first cup of tea, he invited her to a wedding and, by accident, this started her new career.

'You'll have a great time back here, you'll see,' he said cheerfully. 'Lots happening. There's a dance every Saturday in the hall. And there's an excellent jazz club. I'm a member of that, actually. I play the saxophone. You should come to our next get-together.'

'I'd love to,' she said. 'I used to go to a jazz club in Notting Hill when I lived in London.'

'We might not be quite as good as what you're used to, but we have a good time. And if music's too tame, I believe they've started a hang-gliding school, if you feel like a bit of excitement.'

'I've nothing against excitement but I think I'll pass on that one.' She laughed. 'I close my eyes at the top of the big wheel at a fair. But never mind having fun. My main concern is finding some sort of work to do with photography.'

'No reason why you shouldn't have fun while you look,' he said easily. 'Something will come up. My uncle has a printing business over in Glen Tarry. He might have some contacts. I could introduce you.'

'That would be great. He might have some customers who need photographs.'

'In fact,' he added, 'You could meet him next Saturday. My cousin Audrey's getting married and I'm expected to bring a partner. And the girl I invited sprained her ankle badly yesterday and has to stay off her feet for a fortnight. How about coming along with me?'

'Well . . . ' She'd hardly known him

ten minutes and he was inviting her to a wedding! But she later learned that Connor was like that, impulsive.

'She's marrying Angus McGregor, the vet. So you'll come?'

'OK, then, thanks. I'd love to.'

Success

'Audrey Turner's wedding is going to be a really big affair,' Mrs Norris said happily. She was sitting on Katie's bed, watching her decide what to wear the next day.

'They've hired the Royal Arms for the reception, and they've organised a Rolls Royce to take Audrey and her father to the church. And, would you believe, the cake is coming all the way from Stirling. And the photographer.'

Katie riffled through her clothes. This event sounded as though it would be the wedding of the year and somehow she didn't think her cheeky short skirts that she wore to parties in London would be quite the thing.

She pulled out a long, floaty, Indian print kaftan.

'How about this?' she asked, holding it against her and looking in the mirror.

'Lovely,' her mother said. 'That blue brings out the colour of your eyes.'

Katie grimaced doubtfully as she considered her reflection. Living with the gorgeous Alysha, who was spectacularly beautiful even first thing in the morning, meant that she'd developed a bit of a complex about her own looks.

Her straight blonde hair wasn't too bad. It hung in a shining curtain around her face, but she had the pale, sensitive skin that went with it, which was a real nuisance in summer when she needed extra sun screen.

If she didn't give her eyebrows a bit of cosmetic help, they would be non-existent, and the same applied to her cheeks, although she noticed that since leaving London she'd developed a healthy glow.

She supposed her eyes were her best feature, cornflower blue and ringed with lashes just dark enough to do without make-up, but they hardly compared with Alysha's enormous dark, sparkling eyes and enviably long, thick lashes.

She sighed.

'It'll do, I guess. Not the most glamorous thing in my wardrobe but you're right, it suits me.'

Then the phone rang.

'Katie? Connor here. About the wedding tomorrow — there's a bit of a disaster.'

'What sort of disaster? Has the bride run away with the best man?'

'Nearly as bad. The photographer that Audrey hired is in hospital with a burst appendix and they're frantic. I told them you took pictures . . . Do you think you could take a few snaps tomorrow?'

'A few snaps? I'm sure I can do better than that!'

All of a sudden she felt a surge of excitement. She'd show everyone what a good photographer could do and she'd take the best pictures anyone had ever seen!

And that was the beginning of her new career as Katie Norris, wedding photographer.

Creative

The shots she took of Audrey and Angus were greatly admired. She'd driven to Stirling to buy a handsome wedding album to display the pictures and within a week of giving this to the delighted couple, she'd been booked for two more weddings. These were followed by further requests to take pictures at a twenty-first birthday party and a golden wedding.

'You take such unusual shots,' Connor said as she pasted in the last of the McGillivrays' pictures.

'You're a real artist with the lens.'

'Thank you, kind sir. You're not too bad with your saxophone, either.'

'They're going to love this one of Morag and Jim running barefoot along the beach. I bet it will land up in the paper. People love that sort of thing — it's out of the ordinary.'

'I enjoy taking them,' Katie said. 'I love being a bit creative instead of just the usual group pictures. Although, of course, I have to do those as well.'

She finished the album and started clearing away her things just as her father came through the door, rubbing his hands.

'Good evening, ladies,' he said. 'Hello, Connor, lad. Ah, supper smells good.'

'Curry and rice,' Helen said. 'Ready in ten minutes. Katie, tell your dad your news.'

'Oh, about the flat? Well, I've found a flat in town, Dad, so I'll be moving out from under your feet soon.'

'You're never under our feet, sweetheart,' her father said affectionately. 'Your mum and I like having you around. No need to move.'

'Yes, there is. I need to find out if I can still cook!' she joked. 'I've hardly been allowed into the kitchen since I came up from London.'

'Oh!' Connor pretended consternation. 'Will this mean no more of your brilliant suppers, Mrs Norris? I don't think Katie moving is such a great idea after all.'

'Don't worry, I do a mean beans on toast,' Katie said airily. 'And if you ask nicely I might invite you one night.'

'I'll ask very nicely. But just don't expect me to cook for you in return,' he said. 'Frozen meals for one were invented for guys like me. Believe it or not, I can even manage to burn beans on toast.'

'Oh, I can believe that!' Katie grinned. 'But your saxophone playing makes up for your culinary failings.'

'How about I take you out to dinner instead?' he asked. 'Tomorrow. At that Italian place over in Glen Tarry?'

'Lovely,' Katie said. 'But why not wait for the weekend?'

'Tomorrow,' he said firmly. 'There's something I need to discuss with you.'

★   ★   ★

That night, when Connor had gone home, victorious after a game of Scrabble, Mr Norris remembered something just as he was going upstairs to bed.

'Oh, Katie, I called in at the post office — here's a postcard for you from that globe-trotting friend of yours.'

Alysha had continued to write exuberant one-liners filled with exclamation marks from places like New York, Paris and even Moscow.

Check the cover of 'Real Woman' this week!!! or *Yours truly is featured in a four-page spread in 'Clara' this month!!! Do you think I look fat?!!*

Her old flat-mate had certainly made it in the world of modelling, but Katie wasn't even slightly envious.

She took the latest postcard, which showed a picture of Edinburgh Castle.

Doing a shoot in Edinburgh and staying at the Princess Hotel. Please phone, we have to meet. Got a great idea for us both, Katie!

What idea could Alysha possibly have? Did she mean a job for Katie in

London? There was no way she would ever be lured back to the city and besides, her appointment book of wedding dates was satisfactorily full.

But it would be wonderful to see Alysha again. She'd phone her in the morning.

Connor's Confession

The following evening Katie and Connor were sitting opposite each other in Dolce Roma, considering the menu and deciding between pizza and a bowl of pasta while the waitress hovered over them.

'I'm starving,' Connor said. 'I'll go for a large pizza with all the toppings. And you?'

'A small pasta with mushroom and ham sauce,' Katie decided.

She waited until the waitress had left then turned to Connor.

'Come on, you wretch, tell me what you need to discuss. I can't wait.'

He looked at her seriously.

'OK. I wasn't going to say anything yet, but then you sprang this flat on me. Signing a lease for a year and all that nonsense . . .'

'It's not nonsense,' she interrupted.

'Surely you see I can't go on staying with my folks for ever? I thought you agreed it was a good idea.'

'I did. It is,' he said. 'But the thing is, Katie — '

'Would you like to order some wine with your meal?' The young waiter interrupted them with a wine list.

'A bottle of red? Or white?'

Connor looked enquiringly at Katie.

'I'll just have juice, I think,' Katie said quickly. 'Half a bottle of wine would have me dancing on the table!'

'A glass of red wine for me and orange juice for the lady, thanks,' Connor said shortly and turned back to continue.

'Would that be a Cabernet or a Merlot, sir?' the waiter persisted.

'Cabernet, thank you,' Connor snapped.

'And would you prefer a medium sized glass or one of our extra large — ?'

'Medium!' Connor roared. His glare added wordlessly, now just leave us alone, and the waiter got the message.

Katie gaped. This was so unlike Connor.

'There's no need to be so rude to the poor fellow! He was only doing his job.'

'Yeah. Right. Sorry.' Connor hunched his shoulders uncomfortably. 'The thing is, Katie, I've been offered a transfer to a New York office for six months. It could even stretch to a year. And I wanted to ask you to come with me.' He looked intently at her and his hand slowly covered hers.

Katie stared at him.

'New York? You?'

'It's a sort of training programme. Old man Swigg has connections there and he called me in and told me he thought working in America would be good experience. I'm to go next month.'

'How fantastic! He must think a lot of you, Connor, to offer you that.'

'He mentioned something about a junior partnership when I came back. Depends how I shape up over there, I suppose.'

'You're definitely accepting this, aren't you? No question!'

'I said I'd give him my answer by the

end of the week. It sort of depends on you, Katie. I was hoping you'd come with me.'

'Oh, Connor.'

Katie was silent in the face of this bombshell. So this was why Connor had mentioned wanting to 'go somewhere exciting' when she spoke about signing a lease!

But how could she leave Strathcorn just as she was making a second career for herself? And to go with Connor to a place where she'd know no-one? To a city even bigger than London.

'Think of it, Katie. You could get a job over there in an advertising studio, get some really exciting work again, be part of the buzz of the biggest city in the world. I want you to say yes and be my wife. We'll get married before we go. Get a special licence. What do you say?'

She gulped and for some reason her eyes filled with tears.

'Connor, I don't know. We've never even discussed getting engaged, let alone married. You've never said you were serious about things.'

'Couldn't you see I was? Of course I've been serious about you ever since the day you tripped over me at the butcher. I thought, aha, here's the girl I'm going to marry, throwing herself at my feet!'

'You idiot.' She grinned weakly and wiped her eyes. 'I'm not saying it's a bad idea. I just need time to decide, OK?'

'Consider all my good points! I'm the best-looking guy you've ever met . . . '

'Dream on!' She laughed.

'I'm kind to animals and good with cows . . . '

'True.'

'I'm a brilliant musician.'

'And so modest, too.'

'And your folks like me,' he finished triumphantly. 'So what's to think about?'

He was teasing, but serious.

'I just need some time,' Katie said. 'Oh, good, here's our food.'

For the rest of the evening she steered the conversation to other things.

Impatience

That night, after he braked to a stop in the farmyard, Connor reached for Katie's hand as she was about to get out of the car.

'Katie, I've loved you ever since I met you. I should have said something ages ago and I didn't intend to spring this whole marriage idea on you so quickly. I meant to propose one day with violins playing in the background and a great big diamond ring and all that stuff . . . '

'I don't need that, silly!'

'But I had to speed things up when old Swigg suggested New York. You do understand, don't you?'

'Yes, of course I do. That's not why I'm hesitating.'

'Is it that you just don't love me?' he asked quietly.

'No! I mean, I do, I think. I've just never thought about being in love,

47

about you and me for ever. It's exactly what I said, I need a bit of time to think. And anyway . . . ' She shot him a mischievous look. 'It'll do you good to wait. Patience isn't your strong suit.'

Connor gave a mock groan and held her to him fiercely.

'You're dead right. I'm in love with you and I'm not patient. Will you call me tomorrow and put me out of my misery?'

'I'll try. I'm meeting my friend Alysha from London, though, so I might not get much time to myself.'

She looked at his earnest expression in the moonlight and thought how dear he was to her. But did she love him enough to marry him? She truly didn't know.

'Alysha, that model friend of yours? Well, ask her, I'm sure she'll tell you New York would be a great place for a honeymoon.'

'Connor,' she said suddenly. 'Couldn't we just become engaged, and you go over to America for six months on your own, and then we get married when you come back? If we both want to, that is.'

'There are far too many unattached bachelors around Strathcorn. There's nothing they'd like better than for me to disappear for ever so they could beat a path to your door!'

'I couldn't bear it if you disappeared for ever,' she said, and kissed him lightly. 'Goodnight. I need my beauty sleep and I'm going to do a lot of thinking.'

Connor had to be satisfied with that.

Katie phoned Alysha the following morning and they arranged to meet at McGregor's Tearoom in the afternoon.

Knowing that her friend looked stunning even if she were dressed in a sack, Katie chose her outfit with care.

After wearing sweaters and comfy old jeans for so long, she'd almost forgotten what it felt like to dress smartly, and she selected a cherry red jacket and a grey mini skirt. Her spiky heels felt strangely uncomfortable after wearing flat shoes for so long and, as she was driving the family four-by-four into the village, shoes like that weren't very practical, either. She compromised by wearing long leather boots.

'Hey!' Alysha burst loudly into the tearoom, her arms wide. 'I've found you at last!'

She and Katie embraced joyfully, Alysha's exotic dark looks causing a stir amongst the other customers who pretended they didn't want to stare.

Nearly six feet tall, Alysha added to her height by combing up her gleaming black hair and allowing the loose tendrils to cascade silkily down to her shoulders.

She was dressed elegantly in a long red woollen skirt with a cape thrown over her shoulders and held with a heavy silver brooch. But her glittery eye shadow and the enormous hoop earrings transformed Alysha into a bird of paradise not often seen on the streets of Strathcorn.

She beamed at Katie.

'You're looking really good, girl! It

looks as though you made the right move, coming back here.'

'I know I did,' Katie said. 'At first I missed you and all our mates, but I didn't miss work one little bit and I didn't miss London at all. I'm busy. I take wedding pictures, would you believe?'

'Sure, why not? I bet you take the best ones around. And how's the love-life out here in the sticks?'

Alysha was nothing if not direct.

'Well, there's Connor. But we're just — there's nothing decided. He's a great guy, though.'

It was true. She'd lain awake for an hour after she'd said goodnight but she hadn't decided what to do.

'Connor, eh? Tell me all.'

'He's an accountant. He plays the saxophone. He's really nice, Al, you'd like him.'

Actually, she wondered if Connor would like Alysha. She was probably a bit too exotic for him. And he might be a bit too ordinary for her.

'But never mind me, tell me about you. What's been happening?'

'Wow!' Alysha grinned widely. 'Where shall I start? Skating at the Rockefeller Center in New York? On the beach in Bermuda? Jogging around Red Square in Moscow wearing running shorts in ten degrees below freezing? I tell you, this modelling life is a ticket to a lot of great places. It's too bad I have to work when I get there.'

'I thought you said it was just smiling at the camera?' Katie teased.

'I was wrong. It's really hard work. All the make-up and the hair styles and changing the clothes ten times a day, it's exhausting. But the night-life is excellent and it beats working at Matheson's, I have to say.'

'So what's this proposition you have for me? Carrying your bags across the frozen wastes of Iceland while you model bathing suits in the snow?'

'No, silly. Africa.'

Glamorous

Alysha opened her capacious leather tote bag and pulled out a pamphlet. It showed a fuzzy photograph of a woman carrying a bucket on her head, walking across what appeared to be a stony desert, with *Help This Woman To Find Water* printed in red across the bottom.

'This is Help At Hand,' Alysha said.

'And what's that?'

'It's a group of development workers who go to the very poorest places in Africa and help the people with what they need most. They dig wells, or build schools or clinics. They're an amazing bunch of people.'

'Well, that sounds interesting but I don't see how I fit in. Are you connected with them in some way?'

'Yes. I was chosen as the face for these people. They wanted someone black and glamorous to use in their TV advertising campaign and also someone who would be a spokesperson for them.'

'And you can't get more glamorous than you, right?' Katie grinned. 'Wow, so you're really famous. On TV! When will the advertisement appear?'

'Next month, I think.'

Three Weeks In Africa?

Katie picked up the pamphlet and opened it. Inside was a picture of a child tending some scrawny cattle and another of a woman balancing a long bundle of sticks on her head, with a baby strapped to her back.

'Not very good photos,' she observed, her professional eye offended by the poor quality of the pictures. 'They're not even properly in focus. Which country is this?'

'That's Mali,' Alysha said. 'Help At Hand has about four development people there as well as about twenty volunteers from all over the world — college kids taking gap years, mostly. When they go home they feel their work has made a real difference.'

'So have you been there?'

'No, but Katie, this is what I wanted to ask you. How would you like to come out with me to the South African project?'

'Me? What would I do out there? I can't spare the time to spend a year building a clinic, or digging a well or whatever it is they're doing.'

'No, you daft girl. I don't mean a whole year. Three weeks, tops. You can see yourself that they need a good photographer to take some shots of what they do. The people who run the office in London don't seem to realise how important it is to show the donors what's happening with their money.

'And actually . . . ' Alysha paused. 'I've spoken to them about you already. They want me to go out there and be photographed at that project for their next advertising campaign. I wasn't all that keen but then I discovered something. The village they're helping is called Kliprand, and that's where my grandfather came from. I'd really like to see it, and find out more. Who knows, I might have family out there I don't even know about!'

'I can see why you'd like to go. Sort of discovering your roots?'

'Right! So I persuaded the London directors that the two of us should fly out together, you take some pictures of me admiring all their hard work and I get to investigate my family tree. Come on, Katie, it's such an opportunity!'

'They'd pay my air fare? But they don't even know if I'm any good!'

'I showed them stuff you took when you were at Matheson's. That campaign for the homeless, remember? All those great shots of that old couple who lived under a bridge? They loved them and reckoned you'd have great empathy with the people.'

Katie remembered that campaign. She'd been very proud of the photographs she'd taken and it was nice to know other people admired them still.

But three weeks away in Africa?

'I don't know, Al,' she said slowly. 'I don't think I can just up and leave. I've got two weddings to do soon. And Connor has tickets for us to go to a jazz concert in Edinburgh next weekend.'

'I'm not saying we go tomorrow!'

Alysha said. 'How about six weeks from now? Give you time to clear all your dates for weddings and go to this concert.'

'I'd love to go. But I need a bit of time to decide . . . '

Decide, decide, decide. This was the second big decision she was being pushed to make, and all at once.

'I can't just leave everything. I'm not sure, Al, maybe I should discuss it with Connor first. He proposed to me last night. He's being sent on some training programme and he wants us to marry as soon as possible and go off to New York together. Next month.'

'Wow.' Alysha stared at her. 'And? What did you tell him?'

'I told him I needed time to decide.'

'That sounds like a no to me,' Alysha said decisively. 'If you were really, truly, madly in love with this man, you'd have jumped into his arms and shouted yes!'

'*You* might have. But you know me, Al, I've always had a hard time making up my mind. I do love him, but I'm just not sure if I love him enough to marry him.'

'Oh, boy.' Alysha shook her head affectionately. 'Come on, girlfriend, come with me. We'll have a ball! And you'll be doing your bit for a really worthwhile cause.'

Katie sighed deeply.

'I'll give you my answer tomorrow, OK?'

'Right. But I won't go without you. No other photographer will do!'

★ ★ ★

All that night Katie tossed and turned, a whirl of confused thoughts skittering through her head and making sleep impossible.

Did she love Connor enough to marry him? Alysha was offering a wonderful chance to see a part of Africa she'd never see otherwise, and it was a short break, not a whole year.

Just before she fell into a troubled sleep, she made her decision.

Travelling

'Thank heavens for air conditioning,' Katie said, leaning back against the seat of the coach and allowing the cool breeze to blow directly on to her face. 'Another minute of waiting in that queue and I'd have melted.'

'If this is spring, I hate to think what summer must be like,' Alysha, who, despite the heat in Cape Town, managed to look cool and elegant in skimpy khaki shorts and a pale grey top, agreed.

With the imposing outline of Table Mountain slowly receding in the distance, the coach had left the sprawling city behind and was heading north on a smooth dual-carriageway with pink-flowered shrubs running down the centre island.

On either side the rolling hills were studded with sheep and cattle and every now and then a cluster of white-washed buildings shaded by blue gum trees signalled a farmstead.

Dad would love this, Katie thought. Good farm land always gets him interested.

'Wake me when we stop somewhere,' Alysha murmured, pulling her sunhat over her eyes. 'I'm exhausted. Last night was way too late for this girl.' She slid down in her seat, leaned her head against her rolled-up sweater and closed her eyes.

I suppose that's a talent you learn when you travel a lot, Katie thought, gazing at her sleeping friend in envy. She was also exhausted after the late night they'd enjoyed at a club in Cape Town but everything was too new and exciting — she'd never be able to nod off.

Trust Alysha to find such a great nightspot within a block of their hotel! After the long flight from Heathrow, Katie had been ready for a hot shower and bed, but Alysha had talked her into going for a little walk to see the city before turning in.

'Ten minutes, Katie,' she'd said persuasively. 'A breath of fresh air is what we need.'

The sound of music pumping out from a corner near their hotel drew them both like a magnet.

Inside, the cavernous room was pulsing with lights, dancers and a cheerful hubbub of noise. It wasn't fresh air, but it had been a great night.

Five hours later they'd returned to their hotel and left a wake-up call at the reception desk for seven a.m.

Thoughtful

It was a wonder we made the coach in time, Katie thought, remembering their mad dash to the coach station.

The last time she'd been dancing was two weeks before, at the Glen Tarry Young Farmers' Ball.

Connor had worn his kilt, and very dashing he looked, too. Her mother had persuaded her to buy a long dress especially for the occasion, something strapless and glamorous in shades of blue, but it was now hanging in her wardrobe at home and she wondered when she'd ever wear it again.

The music had been supplied by the MacAndrews Brothers Highland Band and there'd been speeches from the chairman of the Farmers' Association and the manager of the local creamery.

They'd had a wonderful evening, dancing the Gay Gordons and the

Lancers in between some good Beatles numbers, finishing up with Auld Lang Syne and a quick final whirl to 'We're No' Awa' Tae Bide Awa''.

It had been great fun and a far cry from the strobe lights and hypnotic disco beat she'd danced to the previous night!

Thinking about Connor, she felt a flash of guilt. He'd made it quite clear that he was upset that she'd chosen to go with Alysha to South Africa rather than to New York with him. He refused to see these three weeks as an opportunity to take some good photographs in an interesting place and the free flight too good to miss. And he couldn't understand that she really didn't want to leave her growing career as a wedding photographer for six whole months.

'You won't need a career if we're to be married, sweetheart,' he'd said. 'I'd be earning enough for both of us.'

'I'll pretend you never said that,' she'd said crossly. 'I have no intention of giving up my work! I've spent months becoming well-known and building up my reputation around here as a good photographer, and I'll certainly carry on after we're married. *If* we get married.'

'*If* we get married? I'll pretend you never said *that*, so we're quits.'

They'd kissed and made up almost immediately, but she could see he was hurt by her decision.

In the end, he'd left for New York three days before she flew to Cape Town with Alysha.

'You'll be away for six months, and I'll be here when you get back,' she'd comforted, nestling against his broad chest before he boarded the train down to London. 'Think of everything we'll have to tell each other! And I'll e-mail you. We'll only be the click of a button apart.'

'Yeah, right. You'll send one-liners that will sound like 'National Geographic' captions.'

'No. I'll send you lots of lines that

will sound like a girl who is missing her one true love,' she had whispered.

And, gazing out of the window of the coach, she realised this was a fact. She loved Connor and already she was missing him.

★   ★   ★

'Going up to see the lions, honey?' The loud American voice from the seat behind jarred her thoughts. 'Randy and I are heading for the Kgalagadi National Park, way up north. I'm Sheree du Pont. You girls going, too?'

Katie swung round to look at the speaker. A pleasant, grey-haired woman leaned forward, eager to chat. Her husband next to her appeared to be fast asleep, his head back and gentle snores coming from under his soft sunhat.

'Er . . . no. We're not travelling that far. Just up to a place called Brandveld.'

'Visiting someone there?'

'No, we're going to a small village where some development aid people are digging a well and building a school.'

'And you're volunteer workers? That's exciting. My, you're a couple of brave gals.'

'Not volunteering, exactly.' Katie didn't know how to explain. 'I'm going to take photographs and Alysha — that's my friend here — she's just going to . . . er . . . see what's happening there.'

'Well, I wish you good luck. A small village, eh? I really hope there aren't any lions wandering around at night!'

Katie smiled weakly. She hoped so, too.

'Luckily we've booked an air-conditioned chalet at the park.' Sheree continued. 'Real luxury. We'll have cocktail hour, four-course dinners, guided game drives and everything. And they say there's very good security to keep the wild animals out. Myself, I can't abide even a tiny little bug getting near me. But I'm a city gal, I guess. I must expect a few surprises!'

★ ★ ★

The coach thundered on smoothly and steadily. The landscape changed to hills covered in dark green-leafed citrus trees with little stalls selling bags of oranges by the side of the road. Behind, a range of rocky mountains loomed blue in the distance and every now and then they crossed a narrow river, sometimes with only a trickle of water in the middle.

Slowly these gave way to browner, drier hills and finally, countryside with a few thorn trees dotted about the stony, grassless lands. There was no sign of life — either people or animals — and it was hard to imagine anyone living out here.

Alysha stirred and opened her eyes lazily.

'Wow. Look at this desert. Girl, this is dry!' She reached for her bottle of iced water which had grown warm in the hours they'd been driving. 'Yuck! I hope I can buy a soft drink somewhere. When are we going to stop?'

The road, although still tarred, had narrowed considerably and when they spotted a group of small houses on the side of the road Katie assumed it was another farmhouse. Probably abandoned, by the look of the crumbling buildings.

But to their surprise, the coach slowed and came to a stop with a hiss of brakes.

Disbelief

'Brandveld,' the driver announced. 'Time to stretch your legs, ladies and gentlemen. Toilets to the right of the service station, refreshments at the little shop over there.' He got up and opened the door. 'We leave again in fifteen minutes. Don't be late; the next coach passing through isn't until Thursday!'

This was Brandveld? Katie gathered her precious camera bag and the rest of her things from the overhead locker and they stepped down from the bus. She felt as if she'd walked straight into the open door of a hot oven. The heat was almost unbearable.

They waited in the sun while the driver opened the side storage space for their suitcases.

'You girls stopping?' he asked curiously. 'Do you have relatives here?'

'No, we're expecting someone to

meet us,' Alysha said, fanning herself with her hat. 'A man called Mike Williams, from Help At Hand. Do you know of him, by any chance?'

He shook his head.

'Ask at the shop. Lettie knows everyone within a couple of hundred kilometres, I reckon. You can leave your bags on the side of the road here, no-one's going to take them.'

They joined the others from the coach and crowded into the little shop, all heading for the large refrigerated cabinet in the corner.

'No cola?' Sheree's voice rose in nasal disbelief. 'Surely you must have cola!'

'Sorry,' the girl behind the counter said. She sounded bored and far from apologetic. 'We've sold out and the truck broke down yesterday. But we'll have more in by the weekend. In the meantime I can offer you orange, ginger beer and bottled water.'

'Well, the weekend's no good to me, honey,' Sheree said, helping herself to a bottle of water. 'Oh, my. This isn't very cold, is it?'

'My brother just got the generator working an hour ago,' the girl apologised. 'But it's quite cool.'

'I hope things are run better at the National Park.' Sheree sniffed. 'You poor thing, you don't even have air-con. How can you work in these conditions?'

'I'm used to it. It's thirty-nine degrees today. You should have been here yesterday; it was forty-two! Anything to eat for anyone?'

Thirty-nine degrees! Katie swallowed. She was hungry as well as thirsty but nothing looked attractive. A couple of stodgy-looking iced buns, covered with a net which was doing its best to keep some insistent flies at bay, and a pile of thick cheese sandwiches curling at the edges were standing on the counter. Otherwise there were just packets of sweets and crisps on the shelf behind.

'Could I have some of those wine gums, please?' she asked. 'And a can of ginger beer?'

She tendered a hundred rand, one of several crisp clean notes she'd been given by the bank in Cape Town.

'Oh, dear,' the girl said. 'Haven't you anything smaller? I'm out of change.'

'I'm sorry, I haven't.'

'She and her friend are looking for a fellow called Mike Williams,' the coach driver boomed from behind them. 'Says he's picking them up. Know him, Lettie?'

'Oh, Mike? Over at Kliprand? Sure. He comes in every so often. Next?'

Slowly she dealt with the rest of the coach passengers who hurried back to the comfort of the air-conditioned interior.

Sheree patted Katie's arm as she left.

'Goodbye, honey. I hope you and your friend are going to be all right. If it doesn't work out, come on up to the National Park, you'll find us there!'

'Drinking a can of cold beer, I hope,' Randy, who had woken long enough to stock up on soft drinks, mumbled. He was clearly looking forward to the promised cocktail hour at the end of their journey.

'There's Nothing Here!'

Alysha and Katie watched as the coach revved up and drove away. Then they walked back into the relative cool of the shop and stood in front of a small, whirring electric fan.

'Do you live here in Brandveld, Lettie?' Alysha asked politely.

'Yep. Me and my brother, Stefaan. He runs the service station next door. Well, it's just a workshop, really, with a petrol pump.'

'What on earth do you *do*?' Katie blurted out. 'There's just nothing here! How many houses are there? Ten?'

'More or less. But I keep busy in the shop. I knit. Old Mrs Burroughs is teaching me to weave. But actually, Stefaan wants to sell the service station. When we can find a buyer, we'll leave and go to live in Cape Town.'

And who can blame her, Katie

thought. Lettie looked about eighteen and was very attractive, with honey-coloured skin and long dark hair held back with a plastic band. Knitting and weaving couldn't keep a girl like her very occupied!

'Is there any way we can contact this Mike Williams?' Alysha asked, pulling out her mobile. 'He said he'd meet the coach but it's been half an hour and he hasn't come.'

'He's got a mobile, but he often can't get through,' Lettie said. 'Those Help At Hand people are difficult to get hold of. It's the hills, you see. Also, the server mast is very far away so nobody around here gets good reception. Some of the big farms use radios but at Kliprand they mostly just use the old landline, when it's working.' She must have seen Alysha's alarmed expression because she added hastily, 'It usually does.'

Oh, dear, Katie thought. How on earth am I going to e-mail Connor if they haven't even got a reliable telephone line?

Debate

'You're driving over to Brandveld just now, aren't you, Mike? To fetch those two girls?'

Marion Miles was seated at the table on the *stoep*, writing something in her small, neat hand.

'You'd better leave soon if you want to be on time to meet their bus.' She was a short, determined-looking woman, every inch the schoolteacher she had been for nearly forty years. She had a strong, deeply lined face, innocent of any make-up, and shrewd, sparkling blue eyes, with grey hair drawn back tightly in a small bun. Any errant wisps were tamed with tortoiseshell combs.

'I'm going in a minute,' Mike said, seated in front of a pile of files and paperwork opposite her. 'Although what we're supposed to do with them, I have no idea. Apparently one of them is a photographer, but I can't imagine what pictures she wants to take around here.'

'For some sort of advertising pamphlet, I thought. That fax from London was a bit vague, wasn't it? I dare say she'll want us to pose next to some of the projects.'

'Count me out!' he said lightly. 'You can put on your best bib and tucker and show them your school room, if you like. That should keep her happy.'

'Nonsense. You're in charge here and of course she'll want to include you in the pictures. I'm sure you're very photogenic. If you'd only remember to have your hair cut,' she added.

'Ah, Marion, you never give up, do you? But you're absolutely right. I'll ask Fran to give me a haircut this evening. Anyway, think of the money I've saved over the years.' A boyish, crooked smile lit up his narrow face and he ran his hands through his unruly brown hair, which had been lightened by the sun. 'I expect Fran will be pleased to see girls from London, though. They'll be company for her.'

'Head Office didn't say how long they'd be staying. Well, we'll find out when they get here.'

'Mmm.' He turned back to his catalogues, which featured photographs of heavy-duty water pumps, and was soon engrossed in the technical specifications. 'I hope it's not too long. We're all busy enough and there just isn't the time to entertain visitors.'

'Worth A Try'

'I'm looking forward to seeing someone new, I must say.' Marion rose and stood on the edge of the *stoep* looking out over the dry veldt. 'This project is just so far from everywhere. Our Kenyan compound was a lot more convenient, wasn't it? Only ten miles from Kakamega and so green. Remember how good the market was there? I really miss the beautiful vegetables.'

'Have some faith in our vegetable patch. You'll be eating home-grown spinach any day now.'

'That's if the goats don't get there first. I wish you would ask the men to finish the fencing around the plot. It's hopeless trying to grow veggies if the animals just wander over and help themselves.'

'I'll speak to Charles about it. I know he's got all the men working on the wells at the moment. Clean water's our number one priority right now.'

'I realise that.' She sighed wearily. 'There's so much to do in this desolate spot. And I've never known such heat.'

'Well, we knew it was pretty dry before we came,' Mike said shortly. He was getting a bit tired of Marion always talking about their previous posting in Kenya, where they'd been part of a group setting up a water purification station in the bush. As she said, things had been a lot more convenient for the aid workers, close to a thriving little town and on the edge of a forest.

'You can always ask for a transfer. Or take a break at home and then join that hospital project in Nigeria. I believe they're pretty understaffed there.'

'Don't be silly,' Marion said. 'I'm committed to this and I have no intention of leaving until we've got the school up and running. You won't get rid of me that easily, Mike, my lad,' she added tartly.

He winked at her.

'I thought it was worth a try.'

*   *   *

Ever since the first time they'd worked together in the Sudan five years before, they'd often been at loggerheads about something, but Mike knew he'd miss her efficiency and her acerbic tongue if she ever decided to call it a day. She was tough but seemed strangely out of sorts this morning, he thought. Marion was usually such a stalwart, so full of energy and never one to complain about the conditions, no matter how hard.

'Right, here you are.' Marion proffered a shopping list. 'Could you pick up these things from Lettie? We're nearly out of sugar and oil, and we need some fruit. If she has any apples, get those, or oranges. You really should leave now or you'll be late.'

'I've plenty of time. Hang on, what's Charles doing back here? I thought he and Fran were organising the men at the well today?'

A grey pick-up came bumping up the

track and stopped in front of the house with a squeal of brakes. A middle-aged man alighted in a hurry.

'Fran's hurt her ankle,' he called. 'Give me a hand, please, Mike.'

Mike hurried down the steps and opened the passenger door. Inside sat a tall, slender girl, her face white with pain.

'Sorry, I feel such an idiot,' she said apologetically. 'I slipped on a stone and my ankle turned over. Charles thinks it might be broken but I'm sure it's only twisted. It's just a bit painful.'

'A bit?' Charles said. 'No need to be a heroine, my girl, I know how sore that must be. It looks like a football already.'

Mike inspected her rapidly swelling ankle and felt it with gentle fingers.

'It isn't broken, but let's hope it's not a torn ligament,' he said briefly. 'Come on, Charles, a fireman's lift for Fran.'

The two men linked arms and carried the protesting girl to the *stoep*, where she flopped back into one of the cane chairs.

'That looks bad. Put your leg up on here, Fran,' Marion said, pushing another chair in front of her. 'That will need strapping up. I'll find the first-aid box. Pity we haven't any ice. Of course, if the new fridge had been ordered in time — '

She just can't resist another dig at me, Mike thought crossly. She knows perfectly well the fax with the order on it didn't go through to Cape Town when I thought it had.

Officiously, Marion disappeared into the cool gloom of the house and Fran Moore smiled up at the two men.

'Don't look so worried, it's just a sprain,' she said. 'I'll rest it, and tomorrow I'll be good to go — '

'You're not going anywhere until your ankle's better, young lady,' Charles said comfortably, sitting down at the table. 'The wells can manage without you for a day or two.' He picked up the pump catalogue and was soon discussing the pros and cons of the different makes with Mike.

'Here we are, dear.' Marion reappeared with an enormous first-aid box. 'I've found this ointment to reduce swelling so let's hope it works. It's the best we can do.'

First Aid

As the Help At Hand compound was three hours from the nearest doctor, Marion had made sure their first-aid box contained something for just about every emergency they might have in the veldt. Apart from the usual disinfectants, aspirin and plasters, there were broad-spectrum antibiotics, ointments for scorpion stings, antihistamines for bee stings and spider bites, and anti-snake bite serum. So far, Marion had never had to use the latter, but she knew how to administer the injections if they were needed.

Idly, Fran picked up one of the phials of serum.

'Oops, this one's out of date, Marion,' she said, concerned. 'Look, it's only good for one year after date of manufacture. That was eighteen months ago.' She examined the other tiny bottles. 'I'm afraid they're all out of date.'

'Oh, lordy. That's what comes of buying supplies in a hurry, I didn't check. I'll put serum on Mike's list and he can fax through the order tomorrow. Let's hope no-one argues with a snake before the new stuff arrives.'

Marion strapped the ankle expertly and fixed the end with a tiny gold safety pin.

Fran leaned back, her eyes closed.

'Thanks, Marion, that feels so much better.'

'And two of these for pain.'

Fran obediently swallowed the pills.

'Nurse Marion,' she said wryly. 'What would we do without you?'

'Luckily it's not really serious, you just need to keep that foot up. If it were broken, I don't know what we'd do. Drive you over to the clinic in Sandrift, I suppose. Oh, speaking of driving — Mike? Aren't you supposed to be on your way?'

'In a minute, Marion.' Mike rolled his eyes at Charles. 'Stop fussing.'

First Impressions

'Oh, good. There's your lift,' Lettie announced some time later.

Katie and Alysha had both finished their second can of soda and were sitting on an upturned crate inside the shop. A cloud of dust was barrelling across the veldt towards them.

'Mike's brought the Jeep.'

Katie hadn't noticed the narrow dirt road which joined the tarred highway further along. A rusty vehicle without mudguards on the front bumped rapidly across the highway and swerved to a stop in front of the solitary petrol pump.

A tall, handsome man unwound himself gracefully from the driver's seat and went inside the service station, calling, 'Stefaan Hofmeyer! Where are you, you old loafer?'

He came out with a young man,

obviously Lettie's brother, his hand clapped on his shoulder.

The two of them were laughing at some joke.

'Fill her up?' Stefaan asked. 'Oil? Water?'

'The works, I suppose. And two twenty-kilo containers of gas, please. Stick 'em in the back but leave space for some groceries. I'll just check with Lettie if those two British birds have arrived.'

'He's talking about *us*?' Alysha stood up indignantly. 'British birds, indeed.' She walked out of the little shop and met Mike as he came towards them. '*I'm* one of the birds, Mr Williams,' she said coolly. 'Alysha Mabenda. How do you do?'

'Fine, thanks.' Mike Williams was not at all thrown by the sight of Alysha, nearly six feet tall, with a figure to die for and wearing very brief shorts. He held out his hand and shook Alysha's firmly.

'Did you have a good trip?'

'Yes. Actually, we sort of expected you to be here to meet us. The coach left here an hour ago.'

'Sorry, there was an emergency, but I'm sure Lettie entertained you,' he said easily. 'Please, call me Mike. Now, isn't there another one of you?'

Katie stepped forward.

'Katie Norris,' she said, and shook his hand. His gaze was friendly enough but distant.

'OK, ladies, hop in. Bung your gear in the back. I'll just pick up the post and some stuff we need and then we'll be off.'

'The last of the real gentlemen,' Alysha muttered, picking up her suit-case and heaving it into the Jeep. 'This one's been in the bush for too long, if you ask me.'

Katie couldn't hold back a little smile. Alysha was accustomed to men almost falling over themselves to do things for her and it was probably a very long time since she'd carried her own bags.

'You sit in the front with him,' Katie whispered. 'Your legs are longer than mine.'

Quite honestly, Mike didn't look like an easy man to talk to and she'd be happy watching the passing countryside. The girls made themselves as comfortable as they could on the seats, which were little more than canvas stretched across metal frames. The whole vehicle was completely utilitarian and offered no comfort anywhere, and as insurance against the rough road, Katie folded her jacket to use as a cushion.

Information

Mike emerged from the shop carrying a heavy wooden crate packed with supplies and Lettie followed him with two big net bags of oranges, which she dumped on to the floor at the back of the Jeep.

'Enjoy your stay,' she said to Alysha and Katie wistfully. 'I'll see you here again when you leave, I guess.'

Mike climbed in and slammed the door.

'Cheerio, Lettie,' he said. 'Be good.'

'I always am, Mike!' she called, waving.

'Poor kid doesn't get a chance to be anything but good in that place,' he muttered almost to himself, crunching the gears horribly. 'She needs something to keep her mind busy.' Then he turned to Alysha. 'Right, well, it's about an hour's drive to Kliprand. Why don't you tell me something about your-selves? Why you've come, for a start?'

'Don't you know? Didn't the people in the London office tell you?'

'They said something about a photog-rapher coming out to take some shots with a model. So you're the photog-rapher, right?'

This was such an absurd thing to say to the gorgeous Alysha that Katie started to giggle.

'I'm the photographer,' she said. 'Alysha's the face of Help At Hand.'

'The face? I didn't know we needed an extra one.'

'They're just using my face in their fundraising campaign in the UK,' Alysha mumbled, a bit embarrassed. 'Posters and pamphlets and so on. Katie's going to take pictures of me with some of the people in the village. And all of you aid staff, of course.'

'Not of me, thanks. I've been known to crack a camera lens,' Mike said. 'You could get some shots of Marion and her school room, though. And the men digging the wells. We're pretty small fry at the moment, you know. I don't know why they didn't send you to one of our more established compounds in Kenya or Mali. Or Nigeria.'

'I fancied coming here,' Alysha said without explaining further.

'Well, I doubt we'll have much time to pose for you. We've got a lot of work to do here, and none of us has the time to swan around posing for pictures.'

'Oh, but you won't have to pose. I'll just take shots while you're busy and you won't even notice me,' Katie protested. 'We won't get in the way. How many development people are there working in your group?'

'Only three at the moment, not counting myself. Marion, Charles and Fran, and we're expecting a full-time vet to be joining us soon.'

'Don't you have any volunteers — you know, students working for you during their gap year?' Katie continued. 'That's a very popular thing to do back home, to go out to Africa or India and help some charity.'

'No, we don't have any of those here. We've only been going for about three months at this particular village and we haven't the man-power. It takes a lot of time to train students to be really useful.'

'But I've seen a pamphlet your head office produced on the work you are doing in Kenya and there were volunteers there,' Alysha persisted.

'Yes, well, at our compounds in Mali and Ethiopia we do have programmes in place for students. There are a lot more permanent workers on the staff there to show them what to do. The students come out and work for us for six months and believe me, by the time they go back, they know what hard work is all about. Some of them quit after a month but those that stick it out definitely benefit from the experience. Um . . . just how long are you girls intending to stay?'

His meaning couldn't have been more clear.

'You mean, when are we leaving? Like, this weekend? Sorry, we're here for at least a fortnight, probably three weeks. Katie needs to get all sorts of pictures of the people of the village.'

Mike scowled.

'Surely you won't find enough to keep you busy that long? I'd have thought that popping off some snaps of the people and the scenery would take just a day or two.'

'It's not just a couple of snaps,' Alysha said. 'I'm surprised your head office in London haven't told you about it. They're having billboards and television appeals and advertisements in the national dailies. Their target is a couple of million pounds, and unfortunately I'm in all those adverts, and Katie is taking the pictures for everything. So you'll just have to put up with us. Sorry!'

'I have to wait for the right light and so on. If my pictures are any good, your head office wants to produce a book about your work here to raise funds.'

Katie tried to sound casual, but ever since the chairman had raised the prospect of the book she'd been secretly thrilled. A book of her work! She was determined to shoot as many pictures as she could and make a success of it.

'A book? For funds? We've never needed one before.'

'Happy To Help'

There was an uncomfortable silence in the car. Mike was negotiating bumps and pot-holes in the dirt-road, changing gear frequently and leaving a thick trail of brown dust behind them. The road they were on was hardly any different from the veldt on either side which was brown, rock strewn and punctuated with twisted, skeletal thorn trees.

Only low, grey-coloured scrub dotted the endless dry sandy vistas, and the heat shimmered across the horizon.

'OK,' he said finally. 'Sorry, I didn't mean to sound unwelcoming. You've got your job to do and we've got ours. We'll fit you in as best we can.'

'Good,' Alysha said, and added wickedly, 'Of course, Katie would expect everyone to wear lipstick and so on, for any photos she wants to take. Marion and Fran, too.'

97

Mike laughed.

'Yeah, sure.'

He turned to grin at Katie, his distant expression transformed by his big smile. She had a feeling everything was going to be all right after all.

'Mike, we'd be happy to help wherever we can,' she said, leaning over from the back. 'I mean, we'd like to be useful in some way. I can't spend all day every day taking shots and I need to get a feeling for the place. And the people you're helping.'

'Useful, eh? Can you handle a pick-axe?' He was teasing. 'Or mix cement?'

'No, but you could show me how to,' she said with spirit. 'And I can cook. I could keep the place clean, and do — um — the washing up. Whatever's needed. Alysha can, too.'

And just in case her friend protested at her offer to cook and clean, she poked her sharply in the back.

'Yes, of course I can,' Alysha agreed obediently. 'Oh, look! Are we there? Is that Kliprand?'

A sprawl of low, tin-roofed buildings was scattered across the side of a hill, almost indistinguishable from the rocky surroundings. There appeared to be a large main building and several out-houses and what could once have been a barn. A few dispirited gum trees hung limply over the house, not a leaf stirring in the heat.

Kliprand

At first Katie thought the buildings were uninhabited, but then she noticed two women sitting on chairs reading. They looked up at the sound of the Jeep and waved.

'That's Marion and Fran,' Mike said. 'Fran sprained her ankle this afternoon, that's why I was a bit late fetching you.'

On the hill opposite stood a large number of round mud huts. There were children playing outside and a few pigs wandering about. Mike tooted the horn vigorously and there was a sudden rush of children running down the hill to meet the Jeep, whooping and shouting.

'Mr Mike! Mr Mike!' Three little boys grabbed on to the open window as he slowed to a stop and asked hopefully, 'Ride?' This was obviously a regular treat.

'OK, hop on.' He grinned. About

seven children ran round to the back and leaped on to a metal rail, holding on to whatever they could for support.

'Hold tight!' He drove off slowly up the hill towards the buildings, being careful not to bounce across the rocks and dislodge his extra passengers.

Katie turned to watch them. Their wide grins of excitement practically split their faces in half and when they noticed her looking at them they nudged each other and giggled shyly. She waggled her fingers, and they laughed. She immediately thought what a wonderful photograph this would make, but before she could dig out her camera, Mike braked to a halt in a cloud of dust and the children jumped off.

They scampered away down the hill and back to their huts. The fact they are plainly dirt poor doesn't seem to dampen their enjoyment of life's little pleasures, she thought with a smile.

★ ★ ★

Katie and Alysha climbed out of the Jeep and looked around the compound. The main house was large, with a veranda round three sides and a scattering of prickly succulents huddled against the walls. Four out-buildings in various stages of disrepair stood a little way off near a large building that could once have housed farm equipment.

'Was this ever a farm?' Alysha asked. 'Could anyone make a living here?'

'Yes, it was a farm. And no, they couldn't; there are more stones than sand here. Hence the name, Kliprand — Stone Ridge. This place was abandoned by the owners and stood empty for ages. We've got a lease on it for five years and for now, it's our headquarters.'

'Hello there.' Marion Miles came down the steps, smiling warmly with her hand extended in greeting. 'You're the two girls from London, aren't you? I'm so glad to meet you.'

She really did look pleased to see them. Her ramrod posture and well-rounded vowels reminded Katie of her old headmistress.

'At least someone here is happy that we've come,' Alysha muttered.

'This is Marion Miles, our teacher in charge of the school,' Mike said. 'OK, let's get your gear inside. I'm sure you'd both like a drink.' He led the way up the steps. 'Oh, and this is Fran Moore.'

A tall, tanned young woman saluted them from the depths of a cane chair in the shade, then began to struggle to her feet.

'Don't get up, Fran,' Marion said immediately. 'You're supposed to rest that ankle.'

'Twisted,' she explained briefly as she shook their hands. 'Marion's got it all strapped up but I'm out of action for a day or two.'

'That's bad luck,' Katie said. 'Have you tried ice?

'Ice? I'm afraid our old fridge doesn't stretch to that.' She grinned, sinking back in her chair. 'Cool is the best we can hope for until the new one arrives.

But I'll be fine, it's just a nuisance right now.'

'Let me show you your room,' Marion said after a moment. 'As Mike might have explained, we've only been here a couple of months so we're not really settled. We've just come from working in Kenya and there we had excellent accommodation with proper electricity and so on. This is a bit different, but we're managing.'

Their room was enormous, gloomy and almost bare of furniture. Two iron beds with thin mattresses were divided by a big chest of drawers on which stood an old-fashioned oil lamp.

Someone had made a rough storage space out of four wooden boxes placed on top of each other, and a curtain rod suspended from the ceiling by thin rope was obviously meant for them to hang their clothes.

The big sash windows opened on to the veranda, which accounted for the gloom, but the room was a lot cooler for the deep shade.

'This is fine,' Katie said politely. 'Thank you.'

'The bathroom is down the passage. The toilet is outside, behind the thorn trees.' In answer to Alysha's raised eyebrows, Marion explained. 'No flush toilets around here, I'm afraid! There simply isn't the water available. But it's perfectly clean, I assure you. So, join us on the veranda when you're ready to meet everyone properly.'

Alysha plonked herself down on the bed and looked around.

'So, girlfriend, no proper loo and no electricity,' she said. 'But who cares? We knew it would be very different, didn't we? This is Africa!'

'And there's a lovely big African spider right above your head!' Katie giggled.

'Katie!' Alysha gave a stifled shriek and the two left the room hastily to inspect the outside toilet, hoping the spider would be gone by the time they returned.

Tension

When they emerged, the group on the veranda had grown with the arrival of a stocky middle-aged man who stood up as soon as the girls came out.

'Charles Reinders. Pleased to meet you both.'

His firm handshake and ruddy, friendly face gave Katie the confidence to comment on his thick accent.

'You're not from England, are you?'

'No, I'm South African. Born and bred in Durban. And don't ask me what a nice city boy is doing in this benighted place because I don't know myself!' His generous frame shook with laughter.

'Charlie's teasing,' Marion said, looking at him fondly. 'He is our Mr Practical. He's our builder, our architect, our engineer and our Mr Fix-it.'

'Ah, don't flatter me, Marion. I'm

just the brains! Fran here is the brawn. We make a good team.'

'We sure do, when I'm on both feet,' Fran said imperturbably, winking at Katie and Alysha. 'Although I like to think it's the other way round.'

No-one could consider Fran brawny, Katie thought. She was wiry, with long, thin hands and fingers, but even while sitting she gave the impression of being physically strong.

Her narrow face was more interesting than beautiful, with lively, deep-set brown eyes which observed the world intently, and her long brown hair was held back with a colourful bandanna.

'Is that a Canadian voice I'm hearing?' Alysha asked.

'Yep!' Fran turned and smiled widely. 'Do you know, you're the first person I've met in Africa who can tell the difference between an American accent and a Canadian one? I don't know why they get so darned muddled. I'm from Winnipeg.'

'Fran's father runs a construction

company, one of the biggest in Canada, and she's been with us for a couple of years, making herself extremely useful,' Mike explained. 'She's not doing a gap year and having fun. She's a very hard-working, hands-on permanent member of the team.'

'I'm sure you are.' Alysha looked at Fran with respect. 'Mike was just telling us on the way here that he hasn't got time to act as nurse-maid to a bunch of students.'

'Volunteers are extremely helpful and we could certainly use a lot more help,' Marion snapped. 'It's just a matter of some people getting better organised.'

There was no doubt about the target of Marion's barb. Katie could sense the uncomfortable tension between her and Mike and she wondered if the older woman resented the man in charge being so much younger.

She reached for the large jug of water which stood on the table. As Fran had said, it was not iced, only cool, but she gulped down her glassful gratefully.

'Did Mike tell you about the work we're doing here with the Namikas?' Marion asked. 'No? I thought not.' She shot Mike a glance. 'It would be nice for the girls to know what we're about, wouldn't it?'

'The Namika tribe were displaced from their ancestral area when diamonds were found there about thirty years ago,' Mike said tersely. 'They were brought here by trucks, along with all their livestock.'

'That's terrible!' Alysha exclaimed. 'There's nothing here! How could they do that?'

'That happens all over Africa,' Mike said. 'Ordinary tribesmen living where there is something more valuable than just grass get pushed off their land by greedy mining companies. The Namikas have a lawyer and after all these years they're still negotiating with the government to be recompensed. But they've lost their tribal lands for ever.'

'For the past thirty years they've been trying to scratch a living from this poor soil. Their biggest problem is water, or the lack of it,' Charles said. 'That's why getting a few wells sunk is so important.'

'Yeah, you should see the water they've been using,' Fran said, shaking her head. 'A little brown-coloured stream that their cattle drink from, and they wash their clothes in it as well. And sometimes, in the drought, that dries up entirely except for a few muddy pools.'

'So what are we drinking?' Katie asked, inspecting her glass. 'This looks pretty clear.'

'Bottled water, trucked up from Cape Town by the gallon,' Charles said. 'But as soon as we have the first well in operation, we'll be drinking the same as the villagers.'

'That's why our top priority now are Charles's wells,' Mike said. 'We plan to dig several.'

'And a bigger school, of course. There was no school here at all,' Marion said, turning to Katie and Alysha. 'The first thing we did was to teach the men and women how to make cement blocks and help them build the school room. That will do for a start. But we're going to add on more rooms as soon as possible.'

'Marion, extra rooms for your school are way down on the list now,' Mike said impatiently. 'Before that, we need to turn one of those outhouses into a proper clinic. Marcus can't keep on using our front room for his work.'

'That's Doctor Venter,' Fran explained quietly. 'He comes across from a little town called Sandrift once a fortnight, and runs a clinic from here. He usually sleeps over as it's a couple of hours' drive back.'

'Marcus is very happy to use our front room. He says he doesn't mind a bit.'

'Marion, you know perfectly well he needs a room with running water, and as soon as we have a well going I will see that he gets it. Twenty children don't need more than one room in which to learn their three Rs!'

111

'If we had a bigger schoolhouse I could cope with more children! Especially if you'd agree to some volunteers to help me. Education is the most important thing we can offer these people.'

'You know what I think about untrained volunteers.' Mike stood up abruptly. 'Excuse me. I've got work to do.'

Danger

Fran watched him leave before she turned to Marion and spoke softly.

'Poor Mike, he's never got over that business with Cathy Thorburn, has he?'

'No, but that's no reason to write off all volunteers.'

Katie was dying to ask more, but Marion said briskly, 'I'd better go and see how Zukisa is getting on with supper in the kitchen.'

'Let me give you a hand.' Alysha followed Marion into the kitchen, grinning at Katie as if to say, 'See how useful I am going to be!'

Katie sat back, looking out across the hills to the huts. The sun was slowly sinking below the horizon, leaving a vivid streak of orange, and blue shadows crept up the valley. The smell of wood fires wafted across to her and the muted voices of shouting children echoed across the field. Cattle were plodding slowly back towards the village, herded by small boys with sticks, and she could hear voices singing.

For a second she thought of finding her camera and taking some photos. But she could do that tomorrow. For the moment, she was just too tired to stir.

Then out of the corner of her eye, she saw a slight movement in the corner of the *stoep*. Was that a pile of rope? No.

'Charles,' she croaked, fear grabbing her by the throat and choking her. 'There's a snake.'

A long, black, gleaming snake was slowly uncoiling and coming towards her with its little tongue flickering in and out.

'Just sit absolutely still, Katie,' Fran said quietly. 'Don't move.'

She sounded just as frightened as Katie felt.

Fear

'A snake? Just sit perfectly still,' Charles said, rising from his cane chair.

'Charles, what if it's a black mamba?' Fran's voice wobbled with fear. 'They have deadly poison and our snake-bite serum is out of date. What'll we do if . . . '

'No worries, girlie,' Charles said easily. 'That's no black mamba. Black mambas are grey; only the inside of their mouths are black.' He leaned down to inspect the thick, black creature which was undulating sideways across the *stoep*. 'My, this is a big one, all right. Nearly two metres, I'd say. But he's harmless; he's just a mole snake. People often mistake them for mambas and kill them — quite unnecessary. They're useful.'

Katie still sat with her feet pulled up, peering doubtfully at the reptile as it glided past, ignoring her.

'He's looking for mice or rats,' Charles said cheerfully. 'He's as good as having a cat about the place. Nothing to worry about.'

Fran grinned at Kate rather sheepishly.

'I can't help it, I'm terrified of snakes,' she confessed. 'I can handle spiders and scorpions but not these things.'

Charles gently encouraged the snake off the *stoep* with his foot and they watched as it moved off.

'He probably lives under the house,' he said.

Katie lowered her feet gingerly

'Remind me not to go digging anywhere around here!'

'You just need to keep your eyes open and you'll come to no harm,' Charles said. 'But you don't want to get anywhere near a black mamba. They're the fastest snakes in Africa and their bite is deadly. Let me tell you a story about my run-in with one of them when I was seven.' He pulled on his pipe, smiling.

'I was out riding in the veldt on my father's farm and I felt like a dip in the river so I stripped off and had a swim. And as I got out suddenly felt a terrible sharp pain in my big toe. So I looked down and saw a big black mamba slithering off into the grass.'

'You were bitten?' Fran was horrified. 'And then?'

'Well, of course, even as a kid, I knew the bite was fatal. But I made a tourniquet out of my shirt and rode back to my dad as fast as my horse could go — keeping my leg up as high as I could. I was convinced I was about to die.'

'Well, you didn't,' Katie said. 'So then . . . ?'

Charles laughed.

'I came galloping up to the farmhouse, sobbing that I only had a few minutes left to live, and when my dad looked at my toe, you know what he found? A big acacia thorn. No sign of a snake bite!'

'What a relief. But poor little boy,

you must have been terrified,' Katie said with feeling.

'The worst part was that my dad gave me a lecture for leaving all my clothes at the river. I'd come riding home without a stitch on!'

'Charles telling you his stories again?' Mike appeared out of the darkness. 'Don't believe a word he says, he's a terrible liar. Here, Fran, I've found you a good stick.' He handed her a long, straight stick, the top smoothed over for comfort. 'You'll need this for a while to get around, I should think.'

'Hey, thanks, Mike.' Fran pulled herself up and tested it. 'Just what I need. I hope Zukisa's got the food ready, I'm starving.'

And with that, they went through to the dining-room. Fran leaning heavily on her stick.

Remote Surroundings

An oil lamp hung low, surrounded by heavy-bodied moths battering themselves against the glass shade. The big wooden table was laid with knives and forks, a jug of water and six glasses.

'Supper is ready!'

A small African woman, dressed in a rusty-coloured robe with a cloth turban wound around her head, brought in a large black pot and set it on the table with a thump.

'That smells delicious, Zukisa,' Mike said appreciatively. 'Another one of your excellent stews?'

'Yes, Mr Mike, it's just stew and sweet potato. And bread.'

The six of them sat down. The scene reminded Katie of an old-fashioned oil painting, with their faces lit by the flickering lamp and the darkness of the room looming behind them. She noticed the white paper serviettes and was fairly sure that Marion was responsible for this domestic touch.

'This is a real farmhouse table,' she commented appreciatively. 'Big enough for ten people at least.'

'This was here when we took over the Kliprand farm buildings,' Marion said. 'It's a good size and will do for when we get some more staff and volunteers.' She looked sideways at Mike.

'Marion, in Kenya we lived with a village of twenty thousand people,' Mike said impatiently. 'We had a staff of ten and about fifteen volunteers, and we needed them all. Here, we only have about one thousand Namika tribesmen, including the children. So we're probably going to stay a small operation for as long as we're here, and you'd better face facts.'

'There's the vet, isn't there? Ryan Norton? He's coming soon,' Fran said, placating.

'He can't come soon enough for me,' Mike said. 'But he's trained in the UK and hasn't much experience. I hope that course he's doing in Pretoria on tropical parasites in livestock will help him become really useful.'

'What's your line of work then, Mike?' Alysha asked. 'Everyone here seems to have a special talent.'

'He's supposed to be in charge of the administration,' Marion said.

'Growing crops,' Mike said, ignoring her. 'Teaching the people which cereals will grow in these dry conditions. I have a degree in Agricultural Science from the University of Western Australia.'

Katie was suddenly very aware that she and Alysha hadn't had anything to eat except a packet of wine gums since leaving their hotel in Cape Town earlier that day, and Cape Town seemed a long time ago. And very far away.

Charles cut them all thick slices of warm bread, and she watched hungrily as Marion served them all a generous plateful of meat and potatoes, then tucked in heartily.

'This lamb is just as good as my

mum's,' she remarked, mopping some of the gravy with the crusty bread. 'But I don't recognise the herbs Zukisa has used. Are they grown around here?'

Mike gave a hoot of laughter.

'This isn't lamb, it's goat. Very tasty, isn't it?'

Alysha put down her fork.

'You're kidding me, right?'

'Nope. Goat can taste exactly like mutton if it's cooked slowly for hours. Zukisa does it all afternoon in our Dutch oven and adds herbs from the veldt. A special treat for our guests.'

Alysha and Katie exchanged horrified glances, but they were too hungry not to carry on eating. It was difficult to ignore the fact that it was goat, but Mike was right, it was delicious.

'Oh, and one thing, girls. Water. Please go easy on it,' Marion said. 'No bathing — strictly washing — until our wells are going and we can rig up a shower. There's a plastic bowl in the bathroom, you can fill that once a day. This house has a small well attached which the original farmer must have dug years ago, but we haven't had it tested yet so we don't drink the stuff.'

No bathing! In this heat? Katie wasn't sure if she could handle that.

'But don't worry, we swim every day,' Fran said. 'The stream widens out in a few places into big pools and there is one we share with the children. The cattle drink further down and Marion persuaded their mothers to wash their clothes in a pool further below as well. The water's kind of muddy but it's cool.'

I'll settle for muddy water; it sounds better than nothing, Katie thought. She fanned herself with a paper serviette, and then wiped her forehead. It was seven o'clock in the evening but it didn't feel as though the temperature had dropped at all. This was going to be a tough three weeks.

★　★　★

Katie wondered what Connor was doing right now. He'd be in New York, staying at the Manhattan apartment that had been arranged for him. She wondered what his office was like and if he was coping with the high-powered pace of work there.

She pictured him eating out at restaurants amidst the hustle of the big city and catching the subway and doing all the city things he'd been looking forward to.

We're certainly experiencing two very different lives on opposite sides of the world. Maybe I should have agreed to go with him, she thought. At least there'd be cold showers in New York!

Katie already had a lot she wanted to tell Connor. Then she wondered how on earth she was going to contact him. Did these people even have a computer?

'Um, is there any way I could send an e-mail?' she asked tentatively.

'We have a generator that runs for two hours a day,' Mike said. 'It's very heavy on fuel. But we connect our computer for a short time first thing in the morning so if you want to send e-mails or faxes, you can do it then.'

All at once Katie was overwhelmed with tiredness. She couldn't help a huge yawn and almost immediately Alysha echoed her. Marion smiled.

'I'm sure you two are ready to turn in, aren't you? You've had a very long day. Don't feel you have to sit up and be sociable. We'll see you in the morning and show you around.'

'Thanks,' Katie said, pushing back her chair. 'I think we will. Good night.'

First Morning

Katie lay in bed listening to the early morning sounds of the Kliprand compound. The sun was already shining and somewhere a distant generator thumped rhythmically. A rooster crowed so close by that it must have been on the *stoep* right outside their room. Fran's voice called, 'OK, coming!' as her lop-sided footsteps thumped down the passage.

A woman, probably Zukisa, was singing a clear, beautiful melody in a language Katie didn't understand, and the rattle of crockery being set out told her it was time to get up.

She turned to Alysha. To her surprise, her friend was sitting up in bed, writing.

'Good morning, sleepyhead,' she said. 'Don't know how you can sleep through all that noise with that bird just outside the window! I thought I'd keep a diary while we're here. Nothing serious, I'll just make notes so when we are old and grey we won't forget what we've done.'

'Good idea. You can call it 'Alysha's African Adventures'.' Katie yawned, swinging her legs out of bed. 'Were you cold in the night? I was freezing until I found that extra blanket.'

'Yeah. I couldn't believe how quickly the temperature dropped. But it's getting warm already, and it's probably going to be another stinker.'

'I'm going to find that washing bowl they promised us before we have breakfast.'

'Are you looking forward to grape-fruit, eggs, bacon, mushrooms, fried sausage, toast and marmalade?' Alysha teased. 'Or left-over goat stew?'

★　★　★

'Three out of seven isn't bad,' Katie whispered later. They'd breakfasted on small brown boiled eggs, toasted

127

home-made bread and genuine English breakfast marmalade.

'I've always insisted on a few little luxuries,' Marion murmured as she passed them the pot. 'This marmalade is one of them. Since I joined Help At Hand I've lived in so many different places.

'In Mali we had a year of drinking tinned milk and the only fresh vegetable we had was spinach. In Ethiopia they'd never heard of potatoes and in Malawi we ate so much dried fish I can never look at another one! Kenya was better but even there one couldn't buy proper oats for porridge. Here we only get fresh vegetables twice a month, so I don't think the right sort of marmalade for breakfast is too much to ask for!'

Katie sympathised. By the sounds of it, Marion had lived in difficult, outlandish spots for most of her life. Her skin was deeply wrinkled and tanned from years in the African sun and although she spoke with a clipped English accent, it was clear she hadn't lived in England for a long time. A jar that tasted of home was a treat she surely deserved.

'Morning, ladies.' Mike drew up a chair. He looked in a much better mood this morning and started discussing the day's work while he drank his coffee.

'The motor of the cement mixer seems to have packed up,' he said. 'You know what I'm like with mechanical things, Charles; hopeless! Could you have a look at it? I'll keep my eye on the well drilling for today.'

'Fine,' Charles said. 'Fran can give me a hand with the motor, then.'

'You fix motors, too?' Katie asked in admiration.

Fran's slim, tapering fingers with neatly manicured nails looked more like a musician's than a workman's. This morning, although her ankle was still strapped, she was dressed in a loose checked man's shirt with work-stained denim jeans and heavy walking boots.

'Sure. My dad expects me to run his

company one of these days, and he got me doing practical stuff almost as soon as I could walk. Don't know how much help I'll be today, though. My ankle is still pretty painful.'

'You really can't put any weight on it,' Marion said firmly. 'Charles, Fran should stay out of action for a while. I'm sure you can fix that motor on your own.' She turned to Katie. 'I start teaching at nine o'clock. If you'd like to come in for a couple of minutes and see what happens in my school room, you're more than welcome.'

'May I bring my camera?' Katie asked. 'That's what I'm here for, after all.'

'Well, if you must.' She didn't sound particularly enthusiastic.

'What can I do to help?' Alysha asked. 'Dig the well? I'm good with a spade!'

She was joking, but Mike took her seriously.

'Sorry, we've five men on the job already. But you can come and watch, if you like.'

'Do you really dig a hole through all

this stony ground and hope to find water?' Alysha asked.

'We don't use a spade,' he explained. 'We're doing something called percussion drilling. It's the most cost-effective way of getting down deep, although it's very slow going. But you might find it interesting.' He sounded as though he doubted she would. 'Perhaps you should change into something more suitable for the dirt and the dust. And by the way,' he added with a grin, 'the Namika men might object to your outfit. The women around here cover their legs.'

Changing Opinions

Alysha was looking cool and gorgeous in a thin white cotton T-shirt and denim shorts, but she got up at once and went to their room. Katie found her rummaging around in her suitcase.

'What does he want, long skirts and long sleeves?' Alysha scowled. 'In this heat? Is he mad?'

'I'm sure he just meant that maybe those shorts are a bit — well, short. Don't forget these are country people, very traditional. I noticed all the women wear long, reddish skirts, and they've probably never seen a girl wearing shorts before.'

Outside, the sun was already beating down. Fran had given in and was reading a book on the *stoep* and Marion was nowhere to be seen, but Mike pointed Katie in the direction of a new grey cement block building down the hill.

'Hop in,' he said to Alysha. 'The well's a little way off, near the river. I'll give you a lift and explain all about percussion drilling.'

'Lovely,' Alysha said, winking at Katie as she clambered up into the cab. 'I've always wondered about that.'

'Cheeky!' He smiled. 'By the way, I didn't mean that *I* objected to what you were wearing. I thought it was very fetching. It's just that the people here are very — '

'Very old-fashioned. OK, I know what you mean.'

She looked at him sideways. Maybe Mike wasn't so bad after all.

Marion's School

Katie made her way down the path to the schoolroom and paused to listen to the children's voices chanting something she recognised. The four times table.

'Three times four is twelve, four times four is sixteen, five times four is . . .'

She poked her head around the door. Twenty children were sitting on the floor in front of make-shift desks and twenty pairs of round brown eyes observed her with interest but the chanting didn't stop until the end.

'Stand up, class, and say good morning to Miss Norris.' Marion spoke slowly and clearly.

They jumped to their feet with shy smiles.

'Good morning, Miss Norris,' they sang, then sat down again like jack-in-the-boxes.

'Hi,' Katie murmured. 'Don't let me interrupt. I'd like to take a few shots, if I may?'

She stood against the wall at the side and waited while Marion continued with the lesson.

Slowly the children stopped being aware of her and turned back to their teacher so she was able to ease her camera out of her bag and adjust the zoom lens. She took what she knew would be good shots, with the children's attentive faces filling the picture.

So this was Marion's school. Surely they needed proper desks or tables to work on?

As if reading her mind, Marion came over while the children sat quietly.

'You should really wait until tomorrow,' she said. 'That's our big day. The desks and chairs will arrive from Upington and hopefully a blackboard or two. It's been quite difficult up to now to actually do any writing, although Charles helped me rig up those work surfaces using planks.'

Katie noticed the desks were made with wide planks balanced on bricks.

Marion was nothing if not inventive. Imagine trying to teach under these circumstances, Katie thought, remembering her own schoolroom filled with bright posters, nature tables, paint pots and reading books.

'You need such a lot,' she murmured. 'Can't you get funding from the London office for more equipment?'

'I've tried. There's a big communications gap, I think, and things go wrong. The minute we started here I sent in a request for funding and somehow the Kenyan office ended up getting the money allocated for us.

'But I'm expecting a big consignment of reading and writing materials to arrive any day. And I can manage until they do, I expect. One must just soldier on, mustn't one?'

Marion didn't look as though she could soldier on for much longer. She looked weary and drawn and this morning she didn't have the spring in her step that she'd had the night before. She took out a handkerchief and wiped her face.

'Marion, are you feeling all right?' Katie asked hesitantly. 'Why don't you sit down for a while? I'm sure the heat must be getting to you.'

'Nonsense, I'm used to the heat. I'm quite all right.'

But she sat down unwillingly, her back as straight as a poker, and carried on teaching from her chair.

Mike's Project

Come on, lads, today should do it!'
Mike stood watching the five men
pulling on the thick rope that led down
into a hole. 'We could be nearly there.'

'Nearly where?' Alysha asked. 'To be
honest, this whole thing looks a bit like
a Mad Hatter's tea party!'

They were surrounded by plastic
pipes and a sea of mud. Two thick hoses
snaked up from the muddy brown river
some distance away, leading to the wide
circle of mud and stones where they
were working. Towering above them
was a tall triangular structure of metal
poles centred above a hole.

A rope was threaded through a
pulley. One end of this disappeared
down the hole and the other end was
being jerked up then allowed to fall by
the men, then pulled up again. Every
time it fell back, it hit the earth deep

138

down below with a faint thud.

'OK, well, I'll try to explain,' Mike said happily. 'This isn't rocket science; even I can understand it.'

'Then I'm sure I can, too.'

'Right. Well, at the end of this rope is a very heavy weight with a sharp metal drill point at one end. Every time these guys let the rope fall, the drill smashes a bit more rock or earth out of the way down there. And every so often we pump water from the river into the hole, let it soften everything that's loose and turn it into mud.'

'Then how do you get that out?' Alysha hadn't thought she'd be interested, but she was.

'Ah, stage two. We pull out the steel bit and lower down the bailer. There it is.' He pointed to a thick hollow tube with a little flap at one end. 'See, we send that down on another rope, and there's a clever little valve that opens that flap and the bailer slowly fills up with the mud and small stones. Then, when it's full, the valve closes and we pull the bailer up and empty the tube.'

'And this has taken how long?'

'We've been at it for ten weeks. Charles started almost as soon as we arrived with this but the ground is very stony. We've gone through three drill bits as well.'

'Wow! You must have a lot of patience.'

Mike smiled ruefully.

'You need it if you're going to work in Africa. Of course, we'd do it a lot quicker if we had one of those electric percussion hammer drills but that's not possible out here. But we're doing fine. Ninety feet down and we're nearly there, I reckon.'

'Doesn't the hole cave in? And get all filled up with sand again?'

'Good question. Nope. We push down a steel casing to hold back the walls of the hole. Then when we reach water, we slip down a narrower casing and pull out the steel one so we can use it for the next hole.'

'OK, this might be a silly question,

but how are you going to get the water out if it's ninety feet underground?'

'Are you sure you aren't secretly an engineering student?' Mike led her back to the truck. 'This is a hand pump. We attach it to a thin black plastic pipe and we just pump this long handle up and down and after about ten pushes, the water will flow out. Well, that's the theory. Let's hope it works!'

Information

The men worked as a team, knowing exactly what to do. They chanted rhythmically as they pulled and released, pulled and released, a beautiful harmony of deep voices echoing across the veldt. Then one of them shouted something and the men pulled the rope right out and coiled it up.

'That's Marundi. He's our head man,' Mike said. 'Charles reckons he's a natural with machinery and he's put him in charge of all the well drilling.'

'Are there more wells, then?' Alysha asked.

'Yep. Five, in various stages of completion. A couple of weeks from now, Kliprand will be transformed. It's amazing what water can do. We'll have clean water for drinking and cooking, washing and growing crops. Vegetables. You name it.'

'That is so cool, Mike,' Alysha said. 'Really fascinating. And you'll have water for drinking and showers back at the house soon?'

'Yep. By next week, we should be all systems go with this well, but of course we won't know how much water we're going to get out until we connect the pump.'

'I can't wait! But I will.'

Alysha looked at Marundi, a tall, middle-aged man wearing only a vest and shorts in the heat.

'Does Marundi speak English?'

'Yes, his English is good. He worked in Cape Town for a long time before he came back.'

'I'd like to speak to him about something. I'm hoping he might know about my family who came from here.'

'Of course. It's time we had a break, anyway.'

Alysha walked over to where the men were standing.

'Good morning, Marundi,' she said, speaking slowly and distinctly. 'My name is Alysha Mabenda. I am looking for my family here. My grandfather Tulema came from here long ago. Do you know anyone called Mabenda still living in Kliprand?'

Marundi looked at her, surprised.

'Mabenda? Tulema Mabenda?' he repeated. 'Yes. Everyone know of Tulema Mabenda. He very clever man, he go to Johannesburg and be a doctor. Then he go over the sea, never come back.'

'That's right! He went to London, where I come from,' Alysha said. 'He worked at a hospital there until he died. But he had a younger brother who stayed here. Tumani Mabenda. I'm hoping to find some of his family still living around here?'

'Ah, Tumani Mabenda. Everyone know of him. He was a big man. Many, many cattle. Many children.'

'Oh, good! So there are a lot of the Mabenda family at Kliprand?'

'No, Tumani Mabenda, he died from the flu. When we come here to

Kliprand, everyone get flu. Many, many people die that year. His wife died. His children died. All died.'

'Oh, no.' Alysha felt a crushing disappointment. She'd so hoped to find some family member still here. Katie had laughed about her wanting to find her roots, but that's exactly what she'd secretly hoped to do.

'No luck, Alysha?'

Mike came up to her.

'No. He says they all died of the flu. I was so hoping — you see, my grandad moved to London and when he married my gran they only had one child, my dad. And then I was an only child so I haven't any other family except my folks.

'It would have been lovely to find a few cousins and an uncle or two . . . ' She smiled, but her lip quivered. 'It's the roots thing, you see. I'd really love to find some African roots.'

'I know what you mean,' Mike said, surprisingly sympathetic. 'Family. It's as though you're part of a tree and you're connected to all the other branches and roots so you want to know what sort of tree you are.'

'Exactly,' Alysha said.

'But I remember now there is Bona,' Marundi said suddenly. 'One son alive from Tumani Mabenda. From a baby, he had bad leg, cannot walk nicely. When I was a boy, we played together, me and Bona. The missionary doctor, he take Bona to Johannesburg for operation and so he was not here for the flu. He never come back because all his family, they die. He gone thirty, forty years.'

'Oh, my goodness. And you never heard from him again?'

'No, never heard again from Bona.'

So a distant cousin had survived, but a cousin who had moved away to a huge city like Johannesburg would be just about impossible to find. Alysha hadn't the first clue how to go about trying to trace him.

Gloomily, she started to walk back to the house. As far as Alysha was concerned, she and Katie could go home as soon as her friend had taken whatever pictures she needed. Tomorrow would be just fine with her.

★ ★ ★

'I'm sorry about your cousin, Al.' Katie came into the room where Alysha had thrown herself on the bed. 'I know you were hoping to find a whole family of Mabenda cousins around here. So you don't want to look for this remaining cousin, then?'

'There are more than three million people living in Johannesburg! How could I hope to find him? I'm not even going there. In fact, the sooner we get on that bus back to Cape Town the better.'

Katie sighed. Alysha was really upset but there was no way she wanted to cut their visit short.

'Al, don't talk like that. I haven't even started taking photos. Why not come to the schoolroom tomorrow?' she said.

'You'll fall in love with those children. Besides, I think Marion could use a bit of help; she doesn't look too well. And Mike says the well should start producing water any day so I need to get pictures of you next to it with water gushing out. We can't possibly leave yet.'

Alysha didn't respond and Katie left the room. But her friend appeared again at lunch, looking her usual cheerful self, and Katie hoped she'd got over her disappointment.

Adventure

They had just sat down to a simple meal of crusty home-made bread, cheese and tinned ham when Mike strode into the room.

'Fran, how's your ankle? Are you up to driving yet?'

'She certainly isn't,' Marion said. 'Honestly, Mike, how can you even ask her? It's still swollen and pretty painful and you know what that clutch is like on the Jeep.'

'I could try,' Fran said gamely. 'Where do I need to drive?'

'Up to Sandrift. We've got a sick baby that has to see a doctor as soon as possible, and Marcus isn't due here for another five days.'

'Don't even think about it,' Marion reproved. 'Fran's not going anywhere. I'd offer myself, but that Jeep is beyond me, I'm afraid. Too heavy.'

'I could take her,' Charles offered. 'Another couple of hours on that motor should see it right.'

'No, Charles, we really need that to be up and running first thing tomorrow,' Mike said. 'I'd rather you stayed and got it in tip-top condition. And that well is just so close to being ready to finish off. We hit mud about an hour ago and I know the water is there. Maybe by the end of the day we'll be pumping. I'd really hate to stop now.'

'What about us?' Katie asked quietly. 'I can drive.'

There was silence.

'And I can navigate,' Alysha added. 'She'll need a navigator, seeing as what you have here hardly counts as a road — it's more like a track.'

'Could you really?' Mike asked. 'If you girls think you can, that would be wonderful.'

'Oh, we'd like to be useful,' Alysha said wickedly.

Mike looked at her.

'Can you drive as well, Alysha?'

'Actually, I've never learned. But I can keep a look-out for potholes and rocks in the road. Unless you need me for anything here?'

'No, the two of you should go together. It wouldn't be safe for Katie to drive alone in case she breaks down. Which I'm sure she won't; our Jeep is very reliable.'

'Just drive slowly,' Charles said.

'I'll draw you a map. Sandrift's only ninety kilometres so as soon as you've finished lunch, you could make a start.'

Ninety kilometres! Katie remembered the Jeep and how uncomfortable it had been. But she was committed now.

Mike sat down and drew a rough map on a paper serviette.

'It's a straight road all the way until you come to a fork. Be sure to take the left side,' he said cheerfully. 'Otherwise you'll head out into the desert and we'll never hear from you again.' He saw Alysha's horrified glance and added, 'Joke. You'll be fine. Just watch out for those potholes. And don't run over any tortoises; they're protected wildlife.'

'Are you sure these two can manage, Mike?' Charles sounded concerned. 'It's a bit much to expect — '

'Of course they can. I'm sure they'll enjoy the chance to help the locals and see first hand how things work.'

'Good idea,' Alysha said. 'Come on, girl, finish your lunch.'

★　★　★

When they went outside the mother and her baby were already on the back seat, the baby wrapped head to toe in a blanket. The mother smiled shyly at Katie as they climbed up into the Jeep, and continued to rock the infant, singing softly under her breath.

'What's wrong with the baby, Mike?' Katie asked.

'I don't know. She has a very high fever and she's been vomiting for two days. The mother didn't tell me about it until this morning. She hasn't responded to junior aspirin and that's all we have, unfortunately. I must ask Marcus to leave us some more basic medicines that we can use until he comes.'

Katie started the motor and for the first time remembered that Marion had mentioned a clutch. It wasn't an automatic drive like her father's car.

'It's got gears!' she muttered to Alysha. 'I've never driven anything with gears.'

'Shush,' Alysha hissed. 'We're being really useful, remember? You'll get the hang of them in no time.'

'Anyone can tell you've never driven a car! Gears are difficult. You have to push the clutch and move this gear stick thingy at the same time. I can't do this.'

'Yes, you can.' Alysha smiled brightly at Mike. 'See you later. And remember to keep supper for us!'

'Of course. And have a treat on me,' Mike said, pressing a note into her hand. 'When you get to Sandrift, buy yourselves a cold drink. And there's bottled water in the back.'

'How will we know where the clinic is?' Katie asked.

'You can't miss it. Sandrift is one street wide and if you drive too fast you'll drive right through. Just look for the grey building on the right next to the shop that says *Clinic* on the wall.'

'Right. Well . . . bye!'

Marion and Fran waved to them from the *stoep* as Katie let out the clutch and they lurched off down the road in a cloud of dust.

'This could be an adventure,' she said brightly, trying to keep the tremor out of her voice.

'Sure. We always wanted to see the real Africa, didn't we? It's going to be fun,' Alysha said, gripping the front dashboard as they bumped over the stony track.

Both girls dissolved in hysterical laughter as Katie clashed the gears with a horrible grinding sound.

'Yep,' Katie said. 'Ninety kilometres of fun!'

'Doing Wonderfully'

Once Katie had got the hang of changing gears on the Jeep, the two girls relaxed and started to enjoy the journey. The dirt road to Sandrift was stony and potholed, but Katie drove slowly and avoided the worst of the bumps, thinking of the mother and baby in the back.

'We don't even know her name,' Alysha murmured, and turned round to their passenger. 'I am Alysha,' she said loudly, pointing to herself. 'That is Katie. And you?' She pointed to the woman, who dissolved in giggles.

'Evelyn Owamba,' she said softly, looking down.

'Well, don't worry, Mrs Owamba, we'll soon be at the clinic,' Alysha said comfortingly, but it was clear the woman didn't understand English and that was the end of the conversation.

'I wish I could speak Namika,' Alysha said. 'I never heard my grandfather speak the language and I don't think he even taught my father. It would be great if we could communicate properly.'

She kept turning round to see if their passengers were all right, but almost as soon as they left Kliprand, the baby's eyes closed and Mrs Owamba covered her head with her blanket, leaned against the side and fell asleep herself.

Katie slowed to take the left fork and clashed the gears as she changed down.

'I'm sure it shouldn't be making this awful noise every time I change gear, Al.'

'I think you're doing wonderfully, girl.'

Sandrift

Alysha turned round to check on Mrs Owamba but she seemed to be asleep, her baby's limp hand poking out from the blanket like a little brown starfish. Alysha took it in her own.

'This baby's so hot, she must have a terrible fever,' she murmured anxiously. 'I hope we get to that doctor in time.'

'I don't think Marion's well, either,' Katie said. 'She keeps saying she's fine but I've noticed her holding her tummy when she thinks no-one's looking. I wonder what they do if someone gets really sick? I mean, Doctor Venter runs a clinic, but how far away is the nearest proper hospital?'

'Let's hope we never have to find out,' Alysha said.

The baby started crying again, a thin reedy sound, and her mother started shushing her anxiously.

'How long before we reach Sandrift?' Alysha asked uneasily. 'Can't you go a bit faster?'

'On this awful road? I'm going as fast as I can,' Katie said. 'But it can't be far now, we've been going nearly two hours.'

They drove on in worried silence, and eventually a huddle of trees and low buildings in the distance became the small town of Sandrift.

Mike was right, it was only one street wide with a few shops and houses on either side. Big pepper trees hung down and formed pools of shade outside the building marked *Clinic*, where some dusty Jeeps were parked. Katie drew up next to them and braked abruptly, waking their passengers.

'Come on, let's find that doctor,' Alysha said, leading the way up the steps and through the doors. 'I'm going to make sure he sees her right away. I think this baby's pretty sick.'

Introductions

Inside it was mercifully cool and only a few people were waiting on the first row of benches in the front room. Most of them looked like farm workers, sitting patiently and talking in low voices.

Katie couldn't help noticing one elderly woman, whose face was smeared with reddish clay, sitting directly below the *No Smoking* sign and puffing on a long pipe.

Katie surreptitiously took a few shots as Alysha went up to the reception desk, thankful that she'd remembered to put her small digital camera in her bag in case she came across an interesting subject.

'The nurse says Doctor Venter will see Mrs Owamba now,' Alysha said, coming up behind her. 'Let's wait and hear what he says. I'd like to meet him, wouldn't you?'

They sat down on the wide wooden bench, worn smooth from years of waiting patients, and watched the door. After a while it opened and a tall, white-haired man came out and looked across the waiting-room.

'Are you the folk from Kliprand?' he said. 'Katie and Alysha? I'm Marcus Venter, good to meet you.'

His white coat was the only indication that Marcus Venter was a doctor. A red baseball cap was jammed on top of a thatch of white hair, and he was wearing a pair of khaki shorts and sturdy farm boots without socks, but his deep-set, piercing blue eyes looked sharply intelligent.

'How do you know our names?' Alysha asked, puzzled.

'Mike phoned and told me to look out for the two of you. I think he was worried about letting you drive all this way on your own.'

'How's the baby?' she asked anxiously.

'I'm going to keep her overnight for observation,' Dr Venter said. 'I want to be sure this high temperature doesn't turn out to be enteric fever. If she responds to the antibiotics I've given her and doesn't develop a rash, then she'll be fine.'

'So Mrs Owamba won't be coming back with us,' Katie said. 'How will she get home then?'

'I can arrange a lift for her with one of the farmers who live in that direction,' Marcus said easily. 'There's always someone with a truck.

'Well, I expect I'll see you both when I'm at Kliprand next week, then. I hear you've come out to take photographs of the work they're doing there.'

'Katie is,' Alysha said. She was struck with a thought. 'Doctor Venter — Marcus — have you ever come across anyone called Mabenda? Bona Mabenda? Or anyone else with that surname?'

He considered.

'Can't say I have, that I recall.'

'That's my surname,' she explained. 'My grandfather came from around here and I'm hoping to find a relative.

But it's a bit hopeless, I suppose; they've all died or moved away.'

'I'll keep my ears open,' he said. 'You never know. I get to meet a lot of people on my rounds.'

* * *

'I love to go a-wandering, along the mountain track . . . ' Alysha warbled. 'Not that there's a mountain in sight, but you must admit this trip has been fun. Makes me feel like one of those intrepid African adventurers, going off into the great unknown!'

'Unknown is right. Do you realise we haven't seen a soul since we left Sandrift? Not a single car or truck.'

'Don't worry, Katie, we'll be fine. And guess what — I've found a packet of lemon creams under the seat. Must be Mike's secret stash!'

'Good. Lemon creams will just have to hold us together until supper time.'

Then there was a sudden, terrifying bang.

The Jeep took on a life of its own and swerved violently across the road. Katie tightened her grip on the steering wheel and slammed on the brakes, which had the immediate effect of swinging the Jeep wildly to the other side and sending them bumping off into the veldt. They came to an abrupt halt at an odd angle against a large rock, their hearts beating wildly.

Congratulations

'Tea, Fran?' Marion put down her book and rose stiffly from her chair. 'I wonder where the men have got to? I won't wait, I'll make a fresh pot when they come back.'

The two of them had finished their first cup when the truck came roaring up and braked to a noisy halt in front of them.

Mike and Charles jumped out, both heavily splattered with mud but beaming triumphantly.

'Success!' Charles said. 'We have water!'

'And lots of it,' Mike said. 'I think we've hit an underground stream. You've never seen such beautiful, clear, cold water. Here . . . ' He stretched up into the truck and brought down a plastic container. 'Taste this.'

Smiling, Marion poured a glass and

lifted it to the light like a wine connoisseur.

'Good colour,' she teased. 'Excellent nose. A promising little vintage . . . '

'Drink it, woman!' Charles commanded. His ruddy face was glowing with satisfaction. Nearly three months of methodical thumping and scraping had paid off handsomely. 'We filled all the jerry cans we could find for the men,' he said. 'I think it's the first time many of them have seen water this clear.'

'I'm sure Marcus will be pleased,' Fran put in. 'He'll see a big drop in the numbers of upset tummies for the children, I'm sure. Congratulations, Charlie, this is wonderful.'

'It was like a miracle,' Charles said.

'The second well should be coming on line in a few days. The men are so excited, now they can see what we've been aiming at.' Mike was pacing about the veranda with excitement himself. 'Now they can begin planting vegetables. And crops. I've got all that maize seed from Australia to try out, it should be perfect for these conditions. We can really start to make a difference here with water.'

Mike and Charles took towels and a change of clothes and went off to the pool to clean up, then came back in high spirits after their swim.

'I think today calls for a beer, don't you?'

Where Are They?

It was dusk, and all four of them sat on the veranda, enjoying the slight breeze. The sound of voices and laughter drifted across the valley and lights from little fires started to twinkle on the hillside opposite, as the Namika people cooked their evening meal outside their huts.

'And this time next week these will be cold ones.' Mike popped the cans open and handed them around. 'I had a fax from the suppliers — they're delivering our new fridge on the same truck as all Marion's school equipment tomorrow.'

'Tomorrow's going to be so busy.' Marion sighed. 'All those desks and chairs have to be off-loaded and arranged.'

'It's what you've been waiting for, isn't it?' Charles said. 'I'll get a few of the men to give you a hand when the truck arrives.'

'Speaking of arriving, where are Katie and Alysha?' Fran asked. 'It's after seven. They should be back by now, even if Katie drove slowly.'

Charles looked at his watch.

'Did Marcus phone to tell you what time they left Sandrift, Marion?'

Marion was silent. He glanced up and saw her face white, and her lips drawn tight.

'Marion? What's wrong?' Charles jumped up and came round the table to take her hand.

'Just a little pain,' she said through gritted teeth. 'But it's nothing. I'm fine.' She patted Charles's hand gently. 'A touch of indigestion, that's all. I'll take something for it.'

She stood up determinedly and went inside, leaving the others extremely concerned.

'She hasn't been right for a few days now,' Fran muttered. 'I think she's been getting this pain quite often but is trying to ignore it. You know what she's like — her stiff upper lip won't allow her to tell anyone she's feeling poorly.'

'She must let Marcus examine her when he comes,' Mike said. 'How long before we expect him?'

'Friday, I think,' Fran said. 'He usually phones to confirm.'

Just then there came a low moan from inside the house. Mike and Charles sprang up and went inside as Fran struggled to her feet.

Marion was lying on her bed, her legs drawn up in agony.

'Sorry,' she muttered. 'It's just — a bit painful.'

'We have to get you to a doctor right now,' Mike said. 'This looks like an emergency. A burst appendix, or something.'

'It can't be that.' Marion gasped. 'Mine was removed when I was a child. I've had spasms of — er — discomfort on and off during the last couple of weeks. But never as bad as this.'

She gripped Fran's hand.

'We're going to call Marcus,' Fran said. 'He could be over here in a couple of hours. I'm sure he'll come when we say it's an emergency.'

'I reckon we should take Marion to him instead,' Charles said abruptly. 'No messing about.' They stood in an anxious circle around her, concern etched on their faces.

'Definitely not,' Marion said. 'I don't think I could bear a trip in the truck, I'm sorry. Not on those roads. I'll just take some more painkillers and see how I am in the morning. It's getting better already.'

'We'll use the Jeep and put blankets in the back,' Charles said. 'That will be fine. Oh, no . . . Katie and Alysha have the Jeep, haven't they? Where *are* those girls?'

'What Happened?'

He went outside, straining his ears to hear the sound of an engine, but there was nothing.

'They couldn't have got lost, could they?' He voiced his concerns to Mike, who had followed him. 'What if they've had a breakdown?'

'Of course they're not lost,' Mike snapped. 'Two grown girls can follow that straight road pretty easily, I would think. And there's nothing mechanical wrong with the Jeep, unless Katie's managed to mess up the clutch completely.'

'Let's phone Marcus and see what he suggests,' Charles said. He went back into the house and dialled the doctor's number but there was no reply. Then he tried his mobile but was answered by a shrill, continuous beep.

Mike stood, undecided, then announced, 'I'm going to fetch Marcus and I'll probably pass those girls on the way. No doubt Katie stopped to take a picture of a flower, or some nonsense. I just hope Marion's condition doesn't get any worse while I'm gone.'

He snatched up the keys and strode off into the darkness. Charles stood watching as the tail lights disappeared rapidly down the road.

* * *

'What happened? That sounded like a gun shot,' Alysha said shakily. Her hands were trembling.

'I think we had a blow-out,' Katie said, opening the door and sliding to the ground. 'Yes. Look, this front tyre, it's completely shredded.' She straightened up. 'We'll have to wait until someone comes along to help. That shouldn't be too long.'

She went round the back.

'At least we have a spare tyre, so we'll be OK.'

Hands on her hips, she gazed around her. The veldt was filled with immense silence with nothing stirring as far as the horizon, but slowly she became aware of the chirping of insects and the call of distant birds. Something rustled at her feet and she looked down at a small tortoise making his way through the long dry grass.

'Isn't this wonderful, Al? And look at that tree! What a weird, fantastic shape.' Katie reached into the Jeep and took out her bag. 'With the sun setting behind it, and these rocks . . . this will make a great picture.'

'Katie!' Alysha exclaimed. 'We've just had a near-death experience and you're rabbiting on about taking photos! We're stuck in the middle of the desert with no hope of anyone seeing us — how can you possibly think of looking at a tree!'

'Of course someone will see us. A farmer, probably. And this is really spectacular with all those branches sticking up like arms. I wonder what it's called?'

Katie steadied her camera on the hood of the Jeep and adjusted the lens.

'This'll need quite a long exposure,' she murmured. 'Al, please don't lean on the Jeep, you're making it shake.'

'Shake! Of course it's shaking! I'm shaking! You don't seem to realise our situation! You said yourself we haven't seen another sign of life since we left Sandrift. What makes you think some-one's going to come along now?'

'Calm down,' Katie said, infuriating Alysha even more. 'Ranting on isn't going to help matters.'

'Oh, you!' Alysha stalked off around the Jeep, savagely kicking a stone. 'Miss In-Control. Typical. You got us into this mess but you don't want to do anything to get us out of it.'

'That's not fair,' Katie said crossly. 'I couldn't prevent a blow-out. Which, if you'd ever bothered to learn how to drive a car instead of swanning around the world doing nothing but looking beautiful, you'd know couldn't be helped.'

'I do not swan! Most days I'm exhausted,' Alysha snarled. 'You have absolutely no idea how hard I work.'

The two girls glared at each other.

'OK. Sorry, I didn't mean that.' Katie put away her camera. 'Anyway, we're going to be fine. If it comes to the worst, we can sleep in the car. If you promise not to snore.'

Alysha burst out laughing and sat down on a rock. Katie joined her and they ate another lemon cream while they considered their options.

Fear

'We can't actually do anything,' Alysha said.

'So we'll just have to wait until someone comes along this road,' Katie said.

'Which might not be until tomorrow some time.'

Without their noticing it, the sun had sunk down behind the mountains, leaving everything around them to fade slowly away in a dark blue haze as the evening shadows drew in. Suddenly it seemed to be a lot darker and colder.

Katie shivered.

'We'd better get back into the Jeep. Let's put the hood up; at least it might be a bit warmer.'

They stood a moment longer and became aware of the sounds of the African night. Far in the distance came a long, mournful howl which went on and on.

'What's that?' Alysha asked, clutching Katie.

'I think it was a hyena. Quick, get in and we'll close the door!'

The two of them huddled on the front seat and peered out through the dusty windscreen. They could see nothing at all and sat hunched up miserably, aware that it was slowly growing even colder.

'Katie, what if someone does come along?' Alysha said suddenly. 'We're so far off the road that they'll drive right past us without even seeing us.'

'If we hear something coming I'll switch on the engine and hit the headlights,' Katie said.

'I think we should take it in turns to stand on the road and wave,' Alysha said. 'It would be too awful if they drove past.'

'Right, you first,' Katie said briskly. 'I don't think hyenas are man-eaters, but I'm not really sure.'

'OK. Stupid idea.'

They sat in silence for a long time.

Relief

What seemed like hours later, the darkness in the sky started to lighten and a huge pale moon rose over the horizon, casting an icy, pearly light over the veldt. Every rock and thorn tree was thrown into sharp relief and it looked almost as light as day.

'Isn't that beautiful?' Alysha murmured. 'I wish I wasn't so cold, I could appreciate it more. Are there any biscuits left? I'm starving.'

'Two each.' Katie reached for the packet and a bottle of water.

At that moment they both saw distant headlights coming along the road.

'Quick, Katie! Switch on the lights,' Alysha shouted. 'It's a truck!'

She burst out of the Jeep and ran to the road, looking for all the world like an Amazonian warrior woman, waving her arms wildly.

'Stop! Stop!'

The truck skidded noisily to a halt in a cloud of dust.

'What on earth happened to you?' It was Mike, leaning out of his window, his huge relief masked by anger. 'We've been waiting for you to bring the Jeep back. We need it.'

'Oh, is that so?' Alysha flared back. 'You need the Jeep? We nearly killed ourselves and if it hadn't been for Katie handling this — this monster — so well, we could both be dead. And it's taken you a pretty long time to come and find us, while we've been sitting here looking like meals on wheels for some wild animal!'

'There's no need to be so dramatic. I hardly think a wild animal's going to jump through the window. So what happened here?'

'We had a blow-out,' Katie said, coming across the veldt. 'The Jeep's a bit dented in front but we're OK — that's the main thing, isn't it?'

'You're right. I'm sorry if you think I'm making light of what happened. I'm just very, very grateful that nothing worse happened to the two of you.' Alysha was about to accept his apology graciously when he added wickedly, 'I'd hate to have to phone the London office and tell them their face had been eaten by a wild animal!'

'I'm sorry I ever told you that silly title.' Alysha scowled. 'Anyway — so, you didn't come looking for us, you came looking for the Jeep. Far more important than two girls stranded in the veldt, of course. What do you need it for?'

Mike explained what had happened with Marion.

'We need to get her to Marcus as soon as possible,' he said. 'But she refused to ride in the truck and we need to take her to Sandrift in the Jeep. Let me have a look at it.'

He parked the truck on the side of the road and sprang down to inspect the Jeep.

'Just a little dent and a few scratches in front,' he said. 'I'll change the tyre and we'll head back home.' He winked at Alysha. 'Watch and learn, Face. Could you hand me that jack, please, in the corner behind the seat?'

He unscrewed the cover of the spare wheel at the back and ten minutes later, they roared back on to the road and headed for home.

Mike set the pace in the truck, with Katie and Alysha following on in the repaired Jeep.

Stubbornness

They drove on through the night, their headlights picking out small furry creatures that darted across their path. Once they caught a huge tawny owl in their beam, feasting on a mouse. It slowly flapped its wings and flew off, its prey firmly in its beak. But nothing else appeared and much sooner than they expected, they arrived back at Kliprand.

'I hope to heaven Marion is all right,' Mike said. 'Think positive thoughts, girls.'

He took the steps two at a time and disappeared into the house.

Marion was sitting up in bed calmly reading by the light of an oil lamp, a cup of tea on her bedside table.

'The pain has completely gone. I can't explain it, it's simply vanished.'

The colour was back in her cheeks and she seemed light-years away from the white-faced woman who had been writing in pain a couple of hours before.

'Really? I can't believe it.' He looked at her, perplexed. 'But I think we should still get you to Marcus tonight in case whatever it was comes back.'

'No, I'm sure I'll be all right. No need to fuss.'

Mike shook his head in resignation.

'Well, I'm going to phone him first thing in the morning and ask him what we should do.'

Katie and Alysha looked into the room hesitantly.

'Hello, girls. How was your expedition to Sandrift? And how is the baby? Come and tell me about it.' Marion patted her bed invitingly.

'You're impossible.' Mike grunted and went to make himself a cup of tea in the kitchen.

★   ★   ★

The following morning Katie was late for breakfast. She'd asked Mike if she could send an e-mail to Connor and once she started, she couldn't stop writing.

There was so much to tell him: arriving in Cape Town, their coach trip up north, meeting everyone at Kliprand, Marion's schoolroom, the sick baby, their trip to Sandrift and their accident. She tried to describe the heat, and the fantastic feeling of space and sky, but found it almost impossible.

I just wish you could come here and see for yourself. Everything is so different from anything we've known. OK, got to run; today Marion is expecting all sorts of equipment and furniture for her school and we're also getting a new fridge delivered. It's going to change everyone's lives. You can't imagine what a treat it will be to hear the tinkle of ice blocks in water!

She pressed *send* with satisfaction, then went through to the dining-room, wondering how soon she could expect a reply.

She found Marion furious, eating

nothing and stiff with anger.

'You had absolutely no right to discuss me with Marcus,' she said coldly. 'I told you I was fine, Mike. There's nothing wrong with me — and today of all days! I have to be here to see to the desks and books when they arrive.'

'Don't blame Mike, blame me, old girl,' Charles said. 'I phoned Marcus and he agreed with me, he needs to see you this morning. No waiting. I described your symptoms and he says it could be one of several conditions and you need to find out as soon as possible.'

'And don't worry about that delivery,' Mike added. 'I'll be here — and the girls. We can handle everything and if you don't like the way we arrange your desks and chairs, you can change it all around when you get back. Which might be as early as tomorrow.'

'And it might be weeks. I know what doctors are like. They send you off to hospital and order all sorts of expensive, unnecessary tests. I'll have to go all the way to Upington, no doubt.'

Katie heard the undercurrent of anxiety in Marion's voice and realised the older woman was scared. She took her hand.

'Marion, it's far better to have any tests you need so you can find out what the problem is and let the doctors fix it. If you don't do that, we'll be worrying all the time that you might have another awful attack.'

'I've never been to hospital,' Marion said quietly. 'Not in Africa, anyway. Only once, a very long time ago, when I had my appendix removed.'

'For all you know, Marcus will give you a once-over and send you home with some pills,' Katie said. 'So you're getting all worked up for nothing. Just wait and see.'

By the time she climbed into the Jeep an hour later, Marion had stopped protesting. She'd packed her small cardboard overnight case with a few essentials and several books in case she was sent off to the Upington hospital.

Mike had invited Alysha to go with him and watch the miracle of clear water being pumped from their well.

'Come on, Face, see what we're all about,' he said. 'The men will be connecting plastic pipes and running them to their village this morning.'

Katie's Class

Katie and Fran waved Marion off, a determined grey-haired figure sitting bolt upright next to Charles.

'So what time do you think that truck-load of school equipment will arrive?' Katie asked. 'Maybe we should go across to the schoolroom and wait for it.'

'Yeah, if I start now I might get there by teatime!' Fran said, heaving herself up and hobbling slowly down the steps aided by the stick Mike had cut for her.

Katie collected her camera bag and the two of them walked slowly across the compound to the schoolroom.

No-one had told the children that their teacher had gone away suddenly, and twenty heads turned to the door when they arrived.

At once the children sprang up from the floor where they'd been sitting.

'Good morning, Miss Norris!' they sang, grinning broadly. Then they sat down expectantly and waited, watching Katie and Fran's every move.

'Oh, my gosh,' Katie muttered. 'What do we do with them?'

'Tell them they've got a holiday!' Fran grinned, lowering herself on Marion's empty chair in front. 'All kids love having a day off school.'

Katie had a feeling this wasn't what the children wanted. She clapped her hands and spoke clearly and slowly.

'Put up your right hands if you'd like to play a game.'

There was an uncertain silence and a few hands wavered upwards.

'Your right hands,' Katie said.

'I don't think they know left from right,' Fran said. 'Not in English, anyway.'

'Good!' Katie said. 'We'll teach them that. Fran, remember that old party game where you wiggled your right foot and then your left foot — ?'

'The hokey-cokey? Yep! That was

always fun.' She stood, leaning on her stick. 'I'll do my best!'

Soon the children were standing in a circle, their hands on their hips, giggling.

Katie and Fran spun around, laughing, and the children followed suit. Soon the room was filled with mirth as the children shook and turned, shouting, 'Put left foot in!' and 'Put right hand out!'

Fran was helpless with laughter and neither of them heard the knock on the open door.

A man stood there, fascinated, a clipboard in his hand.

'Is this the schoolroom?' he asked gruffly. 'Delivery for Help At Hand. Where do you want your stuff?'

'Oh.' Katie, stopped, panting. 'I think — um — which side should the man put the desks, children?'

'Put right side!' they shouted. And so he did. He and his two men brought in desks, chairs, two blackboards and several heavy, sealed boxes and placed them along the wall.

'These must be the books and crayons,' Katie said. 'Marion's going to be thrilled. We'd better leave them for her to unpack.'

'I don't remember my own school being this much fun.' The driver smiled. 'Any chance of a cup of tea? We've just driven four hundred kilometres with this lot.'

'Of course,' Fran said. 'Come across to the farmhouse with me.'

'That'll be where you want the fridge, right?'

'The fridge? Oh, yes, indeed!' She hobbled off and the three men followed her.

Katie smiled at the children.

'OK, everyone. You can go home now. Your proper teacher will probably be here tomorrow so school is over for today.'

The children left the school room unwillingly. Clearly, Marion had never conducted a lesson like that before!

A Solution

Charles arrived back from Sandrift alone, just before lunch. He was relaxing on the *stoep* and savouring the unfamiliar pleasure of iced water just as Mike and Alysha came back from the well.

'So? What's the news of Marion? Sit down, Face, you've earned a rest.' Mike pulled out a chair for Alysha, who grinned at him.

'This man had me connecting pipes, would you believe?' She looked tired but happy and Katie was amazed to see she didn't object to Mike's nickname.

'As she thought, Marcus wants her to go to Upington for tests,' Charles said. 'In fact she's on her way right now, travelling in a government ambulance. Sitting up, of course, and cross as a snake, saying she could catch a bus perfectly well! Honestly, she's impossible.' But Charles's voice was affectionate. 'Marcus thinks it could be one of several things but he wouldn't say what.'

'So how long will she be away? She'll be really annoyed that she missed all the excitement of her equipment arriving this morning.' Katie paused. 'We didn't arrange the new desks or do any unpacking; we thought we should wait for her.'

'Marcus told me privately that she might be away for quite some time. If they need to operate for any reason, she'd have to go to a convalescent home in Upington until she was well enough to travel again. It could be some weeks.'

'Some weeks with no school for those children? They'll be so disappointed.'

Even as she spoke, the solution was starting to form in Katie's mind. And the more she thought about it, the better she liked the idea. Why not?

Surprise

'I could do it,' Katie said. 'I'd love to have a go at teaching while Marion's away. Fran could help, too, couldn't you, Fran?'

'Sure,' Fran said. 'Until my ankle's better, at any rate. Not that I know the first thing about teaching, though.'

Mike looked at Katie in surprise.

'Do you really want to?'

'I really do!' Katie said. 'I know I'm not a qualified teacher but I could do the simple stuff and keep them busy until Marion comes back.'

'Well, if you think you can handle it, that's a great idea.'

So it was decided the two girls would teach for four hours every morning.

'There's a whole lot of books waiting to be unpacked in the schoolroom,' Katie said happily.

'Rather you than me,' Alysha said.

'Believe it or not, joining pipes together with Mike seems a lot more attractive than working with those little ankle-biters!'

'Sounds like I have a permanent assistant then?' Mike smiled and Katie couldn't help noticing the look that passed between them.

'It's a pity we haven't a programme for the women, too,' Mike continued. 'If only there was some sort of craft they could do to make a bit of money. I've not seen any sign of handicrafts here.'

Uncertainty

The following morning Katie and Fran headed slowly across the compound to the schoolroom.

'So, how are things with your fiancé in New York?' Fran asked.

'I'm not sure,' Katie said. 'Apparently there are a lot of young people in the same company and they all go out to fancy restaurants every night. And jazz clubs. Well, he plays the saxophone so he must be loving that. But I don't know . . . ' Her voice trailed off.

'And you're feeling ignored?' Fran asked sympathetically. 'You know what most men are like. They'll never get emotional and tell you they're missing you.'

'I don't think he's missing me at all!' Katie blurted out. 'He's met some girl called Andrea whose father has a yacht and a beach house on Long Island and he's been spending weekends with her. And he didn't even mention my news; it's as though he didn't read my e-mails at all. I told him about our accident, and how different it is here, and finding water for the first time, and all he could say was 'Sounds as though you're having fun'.'

'Well, you are, aren't you?' Fran said reasonably. 'You've both moved to different worlds, Katie, to places you've never known. And it sounds as though he's making the most of the city, and you and Alysha are enjoying it here. I shouldn't worry about him.'

'I hope you're right,' Katie said gloomily.

★   ★   ★

As Katie had predicted, the children loved to learn and were models of attention and concentration, despite the language barriers. But everyone seemed to appreciate the effort being made.

Their evening meal was a tasty

mixture of beans and corn, which Zukisa called 'samp', mixed with gravy from the night before and pumpkin fritters flavoured with cinnamon.

'Delicious,' Katie said. 'Who needs bangers and mash if you can eat like this every night?'

But it was to be mainly tinned vegetables, pumpkin and beans for a good long while yet, until the spinach seedlings started to grow properly.

'By the way, Marion phoned from the hospital,' Charles said. 'They've told her she has gallstones and will need keyhole surgery tomorrow.'

'My mum had that same operation,' Katie remembered. 'She was back home after one day and up and about very quickly.'

'Well, I told her you girls were holding the fort admirably and she wasn't to rush back. Actually, I think she's enjoying meals served on a tray and a television in her ward. Although, of course . . . '

'She'll never admit to watching it!'

Fran finished, and they all burst out laughing.

So Marion would be back soon. Although Katie was finding the teaching fun, she knew that she wanted to concentrate more on her photography.

She had an idea she'd been turning over in her mind, but it needed more thought. Something that would keep her at Kliprand a lot longer, and Alysha, too, if she wanted to stay.

An Idea

Everyone was sitting outside on the *stoep* trying to catch the evening breeze, when Katie cleared her throat.

'I've had an idea and I wanted to see what everyone thinks of it,' she said. 'I've been thinking of staying on here longer, and taking not just photos of the work you're doing here, but going all over the area, taking shots of everything. Then maybe these pictures could be turned into a glossy book, and we could sell it for Help At Hand funds.'

There was silence while her listeners absorbed this, then they all spoke at once.

'Brilliant idea!' Alysha exclaimed. She felt suddenly cheered and realised that she'd been feeling gloomy at the thought of leaving so soon.

'That could be a great book,' Fran said.

'So you'd both be staying on longer then?' Mike asked. Alysha could feel his eyes on her.

'I could stay a bit longer,' Alysha said. 'Actually, I'd love to.'

'That's a very clever idea,' Charles said.

'But would it be all right to stay on here?' Katie asked hesitantly. 'I mean, you might need our room for the vet when he arrives. And I'm not exactly helping if I drive all over the place and just take photos.'

'Have you ever counted the rooms in this house?' Fran asked. 'We could put up three vets and give you and Alysha each your own room if you wanted! We have loads of space.'

'OK, then!' Katie grinned at Alysha. 'So, shall we cancel our return tickets for a bit or do you still want to go home when we said we would?'

'Cancel the tickets,' Alysha said with a smile.

Alysha was surprised at how much she enjoyed working with Mike. She was happy to do whatever it was he was doing: testing the soil or coupling water pipes and, this afternoon, sitting companiably together in the shade of a shed, sorting seeds into packets.

'I guess I'm a Jack of all trades,' he said, writing out labels for the packets in his bold hand. 'And you're fast becoming my Jill.'

'Don't get too dependent, now. I won't be at your beck and call for ever,' she teased. 'I'll probably have to go home long before Katie. I have contracts with magazines that I have to fulfil.'

But she was determined to make the most of her time remaining here, so when Mike packed up the seeds and asked if she felt like a walk, she heard herself saying, 'Sure!'

'Right, let's follow the path across the river up to that rocky outcrop at the top,' he said. 'There's a few ancient Bushmen paintings under an overhang there. You might be interested in looking at them.'

'OK. I'm all for a bit of culture,' she said, 'as long as there's some shade under that rock.'

'There will be,' he promised. 'Careful, don't slip on these stepping stones.'

The path was rough and strewn with stones which made walking difficult and Alysha stopped halfway, panting with the exertion.

'I need a rest.' She sank on to a rock and Mike sat down next to her, wiping his forehead.

From this vantage point she could see the sprawling Kliprand compound on the hill across from them, the unpainted old buildings almost matching the brown landscape. Only the gum trees stood out, their greyish leaves moving slightly in the breeze.

'You handle this heat pretty well,' Mike commented. 'Considering you're not used to it.'

'I was in New York once, for a shoot, and it was seven degrees below zero,' she said. 'So I can handle most temperatures! But isn't Australia just as hot? You are Australian, aren't you?'

'Yep. Born in Melbourne. I always imagined an academic life for myself but when I graduated I thought I'd go and work in Mali just to gain practical experience for six months. Ten years later, I'm still here.'

'I can see why you stay. For the first time in my life, I feel a sort of connection.'

'Must be those roots you were talking about. Maybe, deep down, Africa's in your blood.'

'Maybe you're right. I think my grandfather would be pleased. I look at the people in the village and how their way of life has hardly changed for thousands of years, and I'm quite proud to think I'm sort of part of an ancient tribe.

'I'd love to chat to Marundi. It's a problem not being able to speak the language but his English is pretty good. I'd like to know more about everything to do with his tribe.'

'He'd love to talk to you,' Mike said.

'He's very proud of his heritage. You know, we think we're teaching them but we can learn such a lot from them and their way of life.'

'How do you mean?' she asked.

'The African people have a wonderful community spirit.'

'I suppose you must feel you're doing something pretty good with your life.' Alysha suddenly felt envious. 'You're helping people in a meaningful way.'

'Yeah. Well, I'm not a do-gooder at heart,' Mike said honestly. 'I just like to see people's lives improve. It doesn't take much to make a big difference.'

Alysha was silent.

'My job doesn't exactly make a difference to people's lives,' she reflected. 'Modelling is a pretty useless occupation, when you think about it.'

'Not at all. Everyone needs a bit of beauty to brighten their day,' he said. 'Anyway, you've been a great help here.'

Alysha knew he was just being kind.

'So . . . Miss Help At Hand,' he said lightly. 'Let's have a look at these helper's hands . . . '

Mike caught her hands and pretended to examine her nails.

'These look fine to me. Good worker's hands.' He held them for longer than necessary, then turned them over and studied her right palm. 'A very long life-line,' he murmured, tracing it with his finger. 'I foresee many happy years ahead. But my goodness, what's this?'

'What?' Alysha asked.

'A big journey. One that splits your life in half. It looks to me as though you're going to have two separate lives.'

A new life in Africa? Alysha smiled. No, that wasn't possible.

'Come on, lazybones,' Mike said abruptly, pulling her up. 'We're nearly at the top. Time to look at those Bushmen paintings.'

Right-hand Man

'Katie, do you feel like driving me over to Brandveld this afternoon?'

Fran and Katie had waved the children goodbye for the day and were walking back to the house after tidying the schoolroom.

'Lettie's phoned Mike to say there's a delivery of pipe fittings for us.' Fran had started putting her foot gingerly to the ground but was still not up to the stubborn clutch on the Jeep. 'We could be there and back by supper.'

'Fine. Alysha might like to come along for the ride,' Katie said, packing her camera bag.

'You're going to Brandveld?' Alysha asked. 'Thanks, but Mike asked me to give him a hand. Charles is taking a team of the men to start a new well on the other side of the huts and he needs someone to — er — pass him the spanners and so forth.'

'You've really become Mike's right-hand man, haven't you?' Katie teased. 'I'm glad you two are getting on. When we first arrived I thought I'd see sparks flying all the time.'

'Why did you think that?' Alysha seemed genuinely puzzled. 'Mike's a great guy.'

Fran and Katie looked at each other and grinned.

'Well, he is!' Alysha said defensively. 'He really cares about doing something for people who can't help themselves. I've never met anyone like him.'

Brandveld

Somehow the bumpy road to Brandveld seemed more interesting than the first time Katie had been on it the week before.

'Funny how this scenery sort of grows on you,' she mused. 'I used to think it was so bleak and dry, but actually, it's fascinating.'

'You're right,' Fran said.

The boxes of pipe fittings were waiting for them in Stefaan's workshop. He and Lettie were sitting in the little shop, drinking a soda.

'How are things, Lettie?' Fran asked.

'No use complaining,' Lettie said with a small smile. 'The shop's not exactly busy today, though. I see your foot's sore, so let me and Stefaan load those boxes.'

'Would you? Thanks. You take the weight off that foot, Fran. I'm just going to take a walk through your big city here,' Katie said, looking down the wide street that was Brandveld.

She walked past the row of old Victorian houses, all badly in need of a coat of paint, all silent and seemingly abandoned.

Then she came to a house which stood out from all the others.

A neat white picket fence with a little gate edged the garden which was an attractive mixture of smooth white stones, pebbles and a variety of cacti and fat-leafed succulents.

A sign on the wall read, *Dun Roamin'. Emily Burroughs*.

This must be the Emily Burroughs who was teaching Lettie how to weave. As Katie admired the garden, the front door opened and a smiling, white-haired woman came out.

'Good afternoon! Like my garden, do you?'

'It's beautiful. What an artistic eye you have,' Katie said. 'Would you mind if I took a photo? I'm Katie Norris, by the way. And I know you're Emily Burroughs who knits and weaves!'

'Ah, and I know you're one of the young ladies who's staying with the Help At Hand folks!' Emily said. 'Lettie told me about you. I've been meaning to drive over and say hello. I remember Fran and Marion from Kenya. Well, you're welcome to take pictures, of course,' Emily continued. 'But come in out of the heat. I'm sure you'd like some iced water?'

Inside, Emily's house was white-washed and cool. A huge wooden loom stood in the centre of the living-room and rough-textured woven hangings decorated the walls.

'This is wonderful!' Katie said impulsively. 'You made all these? You're so talented.'

'Thank you,' Emily said. 'I've always enjoyed weaving little mats and so on, and when I came to live here three months ago, I found I had a lot of time to do bigger pieces.'

'What made you come here, of all

places?' Katie asked.

'It wasn't exactly my choice, dear. But my husband Gordon worked as a missionary in different parts of Africa, and when he passed away earlier this year the church offered me this house rent-free for as long as I wanted it. My widow's pension simply doesn't allow me to live anywhere else.'

'Oh.' Katie couldn't think of anything worse but Emily didn't look at all unhappy. 'Who's this?' Katie peered at a silver-framed photograph of a serious young man with thick spectacles, wearing a cap and gown. Emily smiled fondly.

'Isn't he handsome? That's my son, Tigger. He qualified in Edinburgh and worked for a few years back home, but this year he's studying further in Pretoria. Something to do with African diseases. I'm hoping I'll see him soon.'

'Why don't you come out to visit us at Kliprand?' Katie asked. 'Spend the day and see what everyone's doing there. I've been helping with the teaching but now Marion's coming back, I'm going to concentrate on photographs for a book about the area.'

'You were teaching? I used to teach weaving at our mission in Kenya,' Emily said. 'Mats and bed covers. We made wonderful African designs and sold them to all the tourists. The group did pretty well from them.'

Katie was struck by sudden inspiration.

'Emily! Do you think you could teach weaving to the women at Kliprand? They desperately need some way to increase their income. They're all so poor — if they could earn some money by weaving mats that would be such a help.'

'Teach weaving again? I wonder how I'd manage that. I'm sure I could think of something . . . Yes, all right. If you think I'd be of some use, I'd be happy to give it a go.'

'That's wonderful! Mike will be so pleased.'

Reluctance

'Emily Burroughs?' Mike scowled. 'Yes, I heard they'd recently moved to Brandveld. How could you invite her without speaking to me first, Katie?'

'But I thought you'd be delighted,' Katie said blankly. 'You were saying how badly the women need some way of making money and she's happy to teach them to weave. And she's awfully nice.'

'I'm not saying she isn't. But her husband is another matter. Gordon Burroughs is an obstructive, interfering old — '

'Mike, her husband passed away recently,' Katie said. 'That's how she ended up here.'

'Oh.' Mike looked abashed. 'I didn't know that. When I heard the name Burroughs — well, I just assumed it was both of them . . . '

'She's here on her own. I think she's lonely and she jumped at the idea of teaching here.'

'If I'd known that, I'd have invited her out here weeks ago,' Mike admitted.

'Emily's a sweet person but she was always in her husband's shadow,' Fran explained.

'He disapproved of everything we did and thought we tried too hard,' Mike said.

'Well, anyway, Emily said she'd drive over soon and see what she can do,' Katie said. 'I'm going to wander over to the huts and take some photos. Coming, Al?'

'I need Alysha to help me,' Mike said firmly. 'Come on, Face.'

Alysha pulled a face at Katie.

'He's such a slave-driver!'

But she didn't took too unhappy at the idea of spending the rest of the day with Mike.

★　★　★

Emily Burroughs drew up in a cloud of dust outside the Kliprand farmhouse at almost the same time as Marion returned from the opposite direction, driven across by Marcus Venter in his Jeep.

'Marion!' Emily was visibly pleased and the two women embraced happily.

'Emily Burroughs! Fancy seeing you here. How nice!'

'Thought I'd come over a day early and bring Marion,' Marcus said, reaching back for his bag. 'Of course, she wanted to walk but I persuaded her not to!'

'You daft man,' Marion said calmly. She looked pale and tired after the long journey. 'I have no intention of walking anywhere for a bit. I'm going to listen to my doctor.'

'She has strict instructions to take it easy for at least a week,' Marcus confirmed. 'They wanted to keep her longer at the hospital in Upington but she insisted on coming home.'

'Come on, Marion,' Fran said.

'Come and sit down. Emily, hello! Marcus, this is Emily Burroughs. Emily, this is Doctor Marcus Venter. He'll be staying here for a couple of days while he conducts his clinic.'

Over tea, Emily was introduced to Alysha and Charles, and Katie was pleased to see that Mike made a special effort to welcome her when he arrived.

He was followed by a thin yellow dog that flopped down at his feet and rested its head on his boots.

'Who's your new friend?' Charles asked.

'This is Simba,' Mike said. 'He's adopted me. No-one seems to own him and he's been following me all morning. I thought we could do with a dog around here. Simba means lion.'

'He looks as though he could do with feeding up,' Alysha observed. 'That's the thinnest lion I've ever seen. But he has a sweet face.'

'And lovely eyes.'

Mike sounded quite soppy, Katie thought in amusement.

'So, Marion,' Emily said. 'We have a lot of catching up to do, but maybe you should have a little rest and I can talk to Mike and the others about setting up that weaving group here?'

'Good idea,' Marion said meekly, getting up. 'I'll see you soon, I'm sure, if you're going to be teaching weaving.'

'You Don't Sit About!'

'I reckon you'd better keep Marion out of the classroom for another fortnight at least,' Marcus said. 'She definitely needs to recuperate. Well, Emily, you're going to start weaving classes?'

'I'd like to try. I've been giving it a lot of thought since I spoke to Katie.' Emily took out a notebook. 'We'd need very simple wooden frames for the looms. Would you be able to make these?'

She showed Charles and Fran a sketch.

'Easily,' Fran said.

'And I thought I could start by showing them how to weave rag-rugs and once they've learned, we could move on to weaving wool.'

'Rags?' Katie asked. 'Where would we find enough of those?'

'I know of a church group in Cape Town that teaches weaving and I contacted their leader. She's got any amount of fabric pieces donated by a clothing factory and she's happy to send us as many bags as we need. So I asked for ten.'

Mike laughed.

'Good for you, Emily! You don't sit about, do you?'

'No, indeed,' Emily said. 'And I've brought a few examples with me, to show you.'

She pulled out a large bag and some small, brightly coloured mats spilled out on to the table.

'These are beautiful,' Marcus said. 'Made just with rags, you say?'

'Yes. The trick is to combine the right colours. These were made by my beginner group in Naivashu before they graduated to wool.'

'The wool might be a problem,' Mike said. 'They don't farm sheep around here. The Namika keep cattle and goats, all eating every green thing they can find.'

'Then we'll use goats' wool,' Emily said briskly. 'I'll show them how to comb it and spin it. And find local plants to dye it. You'll see, this is going to be something everyone can become involved in.'

'Emily, you can't travel more than an hour every day to come and teach,' Katie said. 'And then drive back again. Your little car will shake to pieces on that road.'

'I was going to suggest you come over and stay with us during the week,' Mike said. 'Just until you get it up and running. We've plenty of room.'

'What a good idea,' Emily said, looking delighted.

'I'd love to help with the weaving,' Alysha said suddenly. 'My mum did a course long ago. I still have the mat she made in my bedroom at home.'

'We'll need some strong twine, Mike,' Emily said.

'Sure. Tell me how much and I'll order some from the hardware shop in Upington, along with the wood. They can drop it all off at Lettie's shop.'

Mike suddenly remembered something

and opened his wallet.

'I received this cheque from Anton Moolman in the post. He says it's for us to carry on our sterling work here, so I reckon this will cover all expenses with the weaving equipment.'

Emily looked at the cheque.

'Aren't you lucky to have found such a generous benefactor?'

'Yep, his heart is in the right place,' Mike said. 'He's a great guy.'

'Who's this Anton Moolman?' Alysha asked.

'He's the Mr Big in these parts,' Charles said. 'He owns a huge property along the river as well as land all over the Northern Cape. His farmhouse is the last word in luxury.'

'You've been up there?'

'Only once.'

'You should see his tennis court and swimming pool!' Fran said. 'And the garden is an absolute show-piece. It's like another world, so green and lush.'

'Lucky thing,' Alysha said. 'I could do with a swim in clear water.'

An Invitation

Before she left the house, Katie checked her e-mails again and found another brief, hurried note from Connor.

He told her he was missing her but he was busy, he'd had a wonderful weekend sailing on a yacht belonging to Andrea's father and he was off with the office gang to see a show off Broadway so he had to rush.

And that was all.

At least he's missing me, Katie thought sadly, closing the computer. And then she had a treacherous thought: but am I missing him?

To be honest, she'd been so busy soaking up her new experiences that she hadn't really thought about Connor very much. She couldn't picture him in her new surroundings.

But it will be fine once we're both home again, she thought, and packed her cameras for a photo session with the people of the village.

They'd hardly sat down to the evening meal when the phone rang again. Charles took it and came back smiling.

'You're in luck, Alysha,' he said. 'Anton's invited us up to his farm again.'

'Count me out,' Marion said. 'I'm quite happy here with my book.'

'And I'm happy to keep Marion company,' Marcus said immediately. 'I do enough driving around on bad roads during the week.'

'So you'll get your swim after all,' Mike said. 'We'd better plan on an early start, then. It's over a hundred miles and the road's not so good.'

That Sunday they all packed into the Jeep and had been heading north along a dusty, rough gravel road for well over two hours when Alysha spotted something.

'Is that an oasis or am I looking at a mirage?'

'That's Anton's farm,' Charles said. 'He told me he's planted over a hundred trees. Mind you, he pumps straight from the Orange River so he's got as much water as he needs.'

As they drew nearer, the smudge of dark green in the distance became a thickly wooded driveway leading up to a big thatched house standing in the middle of velvety green lawns.

The sparkling pool stood invitingly to one side and in the distance Katie could see a tennis court.

'Wow! Is this how the other half lives?' Alysha asked, unwinding herself from the back seat. 'I reckon this lawn would support about a hundred goats from Kliprand.'

Impressed

'Ah! My friends from Help At Hand! Welcome.' A tall, slender man in khaki shorts and a blue shirt hurried from the house to meet them. His warm brown eyes were set in a handsome face, well-tanned from years under the African sun.

'Charles, Mike, Fran . . . And, my goodness, who do we have we here?'

He gazed with ill-concealed admiration at Alysha.

'Alysha Mabenda.' She smiled. 'And this is Katie Norris.'

Anton gripped their hands warmly.

'Come in,' he said. 'Iced tea? Cold beer? My wife's made a cake in your honour.'

They followed him into the cool depths of the house.

'And this is my wife, Marina . . . '

A woman with her hair pulled up into

a ponytail carried in an iced cake, followed by two uniformed maids with trays laden with tea, coffee and cool drinks. Marina smiled politely but didn't speak much beyond a quiet greeting.

'Get some refreshments inside you, then how about a little swim?' Anton said. 'Or is there anyone who wants to beat me at tennis?'

'A swim, please,' Alysha said. 'It's far too hot to run around a tennis court.'

'Good thinking. You'll find the pool room outside where you can change.'

★　★　★

The pool was wonderfully cool, and soon everyone was splashing around enjoying themselves.

Katie floated dreamily, looking up with pleasure at the flowering shrubs and towering trees that edged the garden.

Anton himself didn't swim, but sat watching his guests in the pool. After a time, a servant brought out another tray of iced drinks and snacks ready for when they came out of the water.

There was something to suit everyone — fruit juices, iced beers and wine and cocktails. Katie noticed Anton was the only one who drank these.

'I could get used to this,' Alysha murmured.

'Don't,' Fran whispered. 'We have to go home this afternoon!'

Marina served an enormous lunch on the shady *stoep*.

Katie would have liked to chat to her about her life on the farm, but she realised that Anton's wife must be Afrikaans as she seemed to find their conversation in English difficult to follow.

Unlike his wife, Anton spoke perfect English and, in between urging them to eat some more, he regaled them with jokes. He was genuinely impressed that they'd found water in such an old-fashioned way.

'If you're not able to pump from the

river, boreholes around these parts cost an absolute fortune,' he said. 'It's all the rock you have to drill through. I hope the Namika know how lucky they are to have help from you folk. You're doing a splendid job.'

Somewhere inside the house a bell pealed and Marina hurried to answer it. She came and whispered in her husband's ear and Anton stood up immediately.

'Excuse me.' He smiled. 'Business associates. Please, carry on.'

Katie glimpsed two African men in dark suits waiting for him in the hall. The men had an air of authority and their almost military demeanour was out of place on a farm.

In the driveway behind them, a long black limousine with tinted windows was parked in the shade.

Anton ushered the men into a room off the side and stayed away for the rest of the meal.

That's odd, Katie thought. She felt with sudden certainty that Anton

Moolman was something more than just a kind-hearted farmer. The man they called Mr Big certainly had other interests besides orange trees and cattle farming . . .

Amazing Coincidence

'There will be seven for supper tonight, Zukisa,' Marion said. 'Mrs Burroughs is staying with us for a while. I've made up a bed for her in one of the back rooms.'

'And Mr Doctor Marcus?' Zukisa insisted on both titles.

'He's coming tomorrow to hold his clinic here and staying overnight, I expect, in his usual room.'

'House full!' Zukisa said cheerfully. Nothing seemed to bother Zukisa and the more people she had to feed, the happier she was.

It's lucky that we have such a big place, Marion thought, carrying a little pot of dried grasses to put by Emily's bedside. Emily's small suitcase was already unpacked and several bags of colourful fabric spilled out on to the floor. Emily was on the front *stoep*, explaining how she wanted the weaving looms to be made.

'They need to be about the size of a door frame,' she said. 'Good and strong, with notches cut for the warp string to be threaded from top to bottom.'

'I thought they'd start by making place mats,' Alysha said. 'Something small.'

'No point in starting with small mats,' Emily said briskly. 'Once they have some finer goats' wool spun and dyed, we can do those. But we're starting with off-cuts of synthetic fabric and they make thick and chunky mats. Perfect for a bathroom. I know of a shop in Cape Town which sells these; they're very popular because they're machine-washable.'

'Emily, I had no idea you were such a businesswoman!' Mike smiled. 'You're a woman of many talents.'

'Why, thank you, kind sir!'

Emily was looking flushed and happy. She's obviously pleased to be busy again, Katie thought. But there was something else Emily was desperate to share.

'I've had some wonderful news. My son Tigger is coming here for six months. Right here, to Help At Hand! I had no idea he'd signed up to work with all of you. Isn't that an amazing coincidence?'

'Your son?' Mike looked puzzled. 'The only person we're expecting is the new vet. Ryan Norton's his name and he's supposed to arrive some time next week.'

'That's right! That's Tigger! His real name is Ryan but we've always called him Tigger. From Winnie The Pooh, you know. He had a stuffed toy tiger when he was little . . . '

Katie remembered the owlish, bespectacled face in the silver frame on Emily's table.

'But his surname's *Norton*?'

'Before I married Gordon, I was married to David Norton. We were both very young and he died in a motorcycle accident when Ryan was only two. Then a few years later I met Gordon and went out to Kenya with him and Gordon brought Ryan up as his own child. But he never formally adopted him. So Tigger's still Ryan Norton.'

'That's lovely for you,' Marion said warmly. 'I remember him as a little boy. But he was off at boarding school most of the time, wasn't he? In Nairobi?'

'That's right. Gordon didn't want . . . well, he felt that Tigger needed the company of other boys, so he was a boarder from the time he was seven. And the best schools were in the city, of course — those village schools weren't very good.'

'You must have missed him. Your only son,' Katie said. She couldn't imagine being sent away from home so young.

'Oh, I did. Dreadfully. But I quite understood. Gordon's work was very important. And then when he'd finished at boarding school Tigger went off to university in Edinburgh, and after

234

that he went straight into practice with a vet in Dundee for several years.'

'So you haven't seen much of him,' Marion said gently. 'It will be good to have him right here, won't it? What made him decide to leave that practice in Dundee?'

'Perhaps the wet weather got him down! No, he said his heart has always been here, in Africa. Like mine is. And he realised that if he wanted to come back, he'd be more useful if he studied African diseases in cattle, so that's what he's been doing.'

'Isn't it strange how things work out?'

'I've always known that everything happens for the best in the end,' Emily said contentedly, unsmiling, and obviously considered this an official meeting. Simba, lying at Mike's feet, stood up and bristled, growling softly.

'Sit,' Mike said, stroking his new pet. 'These are friends.'

Alysha recognised Marundi immediately. He was dressed quite formally in an old suit with fraying cuffs and highly polished shoes but without any socks, and had obviously come along as an interpreter.

The Chief was dressed in full regalia. Around his waist was a sort of skirt of buckskin, decorated with beads and fastened with enormous silver safety pins. Over his shoulders he wore the skin of a zebra which hung down at the back almost to the ground. The stiff mane of the animal had been twisted into a headdress, giving him an impressive mass of straight black hair standing above his head, and his arms were decorated with silver bracelets which had been made from tin cans hammered into patterns.

'Doesn't he look magnificent?' Katie whispered, and slipped back into the house to fetch her camera. The others set out chairs for everyone and waited for the Chief, who sat down without expression. He said something to Marundi who translated.

'My Chief says that he has been told you want his women to work for you.'

'No, no!' Mike said. 'Not at all. We would like to teach them how to weave mats. So they can work for themselves and earn some money.'

'Ah.' Marundi spoke rapidly in Namika, then listened respectfully to the Chief's reply.

'My Chief says the women already know how to weave grass mats. Why should they need to be taught?'

'These are different mats,' Marion said. 'Very pretty. The women can sell them to rich people in the city. Tourists will like them. Wait, I'll show you.'

She went back inside the house and returned with the small mats she had shown Mike.

The Chief smiled broadly and leaned forward to run his fingers over them. There was some rapid-fire conversation between the two men, then Marundi beamed.

'My Chief says these are very pretty. He would like the women to make these. He says he can see our women will get very, very rich.'

'Oh, dear,' Emily said anxiously. 'Tell him they won't get very rich. But when they've learned how to weave they'll certainly be able to earn something, which is better than nothing — which is what they're earning right now.'

They were interrupted by Zukisa bringing out a tray laden with tea and biscuits. She served the Chief first, curtsying in front of him and bowing her head while he helped himself to a fistful of biscuits. Then he spooned six heaped spoons of sugar into his tea and stirred it enthusiastically.

'The Chief says, good tea,' Marundi murmured, doing the same himself.

The Chief sat silent, drinking his tea and smiling beatifically at everyone. Then he stood up to leave.

'Is good,' he said suddenly in English. 'You teach. They learn.'

'Please, accept this mat as a gift,' Emily said, handing him one woven with red and yellow rags. He took it from her and tucked it under his arm.

'Is pretty.' He beamed.

As he left, they all smiled with relief. So the weaving project had received the official stamp of approval!

Speculation

'So, what does this son of Emily's look like, then?' Fran asked. The three girls were in the schoolroom, tying the warp twine and stretching it tightly from the top of the loom frame to the bottom. 'You saw his photo, didn't you?'

'He's sort of — well, rather overweight,' Katie said. 'Think Billy Bunter. Thick glasses. I guess only a mother would call him good-looking! But hey, he's a vet, he's got to be a nice person. I've never met a vet who wasn't.'

'He'll have his work cut out,' Alysha predicted. 'The cattle here are so thin and miserable; just skin and bone.'

'Didn't Mike say they all had some sort of parasite?' Katie said. 'If this fellow has studied African diseases then he should be able to put them right.'

'I remember they talked about him in Kenya but I never met him there,' Fran said, cutting the twine and knotting it expertly. 'He was away studying in Edinburgh already. Do we call him Ryan or Tigger, I wonder?'

'I expect he'll tell us,' Katie said absently. 'Oh, there's Marcus!'

The two girls watched as the doctor's battered Jeep drew up and Marcus climbed out stiffly, his red baseball cap jammed firmly on to his unruly white hair. He mounted the steps to the veranda and sat down heavily on a cane chair.

'Poor man looks done in,' Alysha said. 'He travels such long distances between his clinics and the roads are so awful. And I'm sure there are loads of people here just waiting to queue up and see him tomorrow.'

'I wonder why he chose to work in such a difficult place,' Katie said. 'He could be at some big modern hospital in Johannesburg or Cape Town, or even private practice, and be making shed-loads of money.'

'He's just kind-hearted, I think,'

Alysha said. 'A naturally good guy who wants to make the world a better place. Let's go and chat to him, see if he'd like some tea.'

* * *

By the time they'd tidied away the twine and stacked the finished looms against the wall ready for the women the following day, Emily was already pouring Marcus a cup of tea. The two of them were laughing over some joke and seemed to be getting on very well.

'Emily here tells me she's a chess player,' Marcus said, beaming. 'And she's even brought her board with her. At last I've found someone who wants to give me a game.'

'Scrabble's more my mark,' Katie said. 'Marion and I often play.'

'We'll set up the boards after supper then,' Marcus said. 'By the way, Alysha, I have some news for you. About that cousin you were asking about, Bona Mabenda.'

'You've found him?' Alysha was electrified. 'Where?'

'No, not found him. Heard about him. I was talking to people up in Sandrift and an old man there remembered your family. He said Bona had had a bad leg since he was small — probably polio, I imagine, but he didn't know — and a missionary took him up to Johannesburg to have an operation.'

'Yes, but I'd heard that already,' Alysha said, disappointed. 'But he just got swallowed up in the big city afterwards, I think. Disappeared.'

'Not entirely,' Marcus said. 'Apparently, after the operation, he lived with the family of the missionary who took him. And he won a scholarship to a very fancy church school there and did very well.'

'Really? And then?'

'That's all the old man knew. But at least you have a bit more information now.'

'Thanks.' Alysha bit her lip. 'So, the next thing I have to do is just go and knock on the door of all the church schools in Johannesburg and ask if anyone knows what became of him!'

'Not at all, dear,' Emily said cheerfully. 'I still have connections with the church. I could easily get a list of all the schools in Johannesburg, and their addresses. So you could simply write to them. They must have names of all their past pupils. Especially those who were on scholarships.'

'Emily, could you? That would be brilliant!' Alysha said. 'There's a good chance one of them would know what became of him, isn't there? Gosh, for the first time I feel I might really find this cousin!'

'Glad to be able to help,' Emily said. 'So, Marcus, you've just come from Sandrift? Tell me more about your clinic there.'

'Very busy,' Marcus said laconically. 'I start at seven in the morning, while it's cool, but there's already a queue waiting to see me. Mostly mothers with babies. It's maddening to see the same old problems presented every fortnight, problems that can be so easily prevented.

The mothers need to be taught how to feed their babies and no matter how many pamphlets the government hands out, if their mothers can't read, what's the use?'

'Lack of education! That's the biggest problem in Africa!' Emily agreed excitedly. 'You're so right, Marcus.'

The girls could tell this subject was dear to both their hearts and they got up, smiling.

'We'll leave you to it,' Alysha said. 'Oh, there's Mike. I'll just — um — I want to tell him the news about my cousin. Excuse me.'

Katie watched her run down the track to where Mike was returning to the house. She couldn't hear what they were saying but Mike gave her a hug and then the two of them sauntered down to the river, swinging their arms together, hand in hand.

Oh, Katie thought. So *that's* the way the wind blows! I thought so!

And for a moment she felt a stab of envy. Why was Connor so far away?

245

'It Looks Amazing'

It was afternoon, school was over for the day and Alysha sat on a small stool on the *stoep* of the schoolroom. She was methodically tearing the brightly coloured fabric into thin strips, while ten Namika women sat on the floor, watching Emily's every move as she demonstrated how to weave the strips into a rug.

She'd firmly rejected asking one of the few women who could speak English to act as translator.

'There's no need,' she said. 'Everyone will learn by watching and besides, weaving is a universal language!'

Her nimble fingers pushed and pulled the fabric strips through the long warp strings, tamping each one down hard before she used the next. She'd chosen vivid reds, yellows and oranges as her colour mix and slowly the coloured strips built up into a thick, nubbly mat on the loom.

'It's so simple but it looks amazing.' Alysha admired her work.

'And at almost no cost,' Emily said cheerfully. 'All this fabric is donated. Just off-cuts from a factory in Cape Town that makes polyester T-shirts. Perfect for weaving.'

Alysha had piled the torn strips into heaps, each of a different colour.

Emily indicated that the women should choose their own colour schemes but they just giggled shyly and clapped their hands to their mouths.

'Like this,' Alysha offered, picking up a handful of brown, yellow and dark red strips and holding them together. 'See?'

Encouraged

The first woman murmured something and hesitantly stretched out her hand towards the red strips, looking questioningly at Alysha.

'Lovely! And now some more . . . '

Slowly they all helped themselves to the strips, faster and faster, until there was almost none left.

'We'll need a lot more, dear,' Emily said. 'You'll be surprised how many pieces go into making a rug.'

Alysha returned to her job of tearing, and she and Emily watched as the women began to twist the fabric back and forth between the strings, chattering excitedly as they did so.

'They know exactly what they're doing,' Emily said. 'With all the grass mats they've made, it comes easily. Oh, I do like the colours you've chosen, dear!'

She picked up the pieces one young

woman had selected, a mixture of cool blues, greens and purple.

'This will look wonderful. And how about a touch of white . . . ?'

She added some to the mix and was rewarded with a huge smile of agreement.

'My name is Emily,' she said slowly, pointing to herself. 'And your name is . . . ?'

'Name is Zola,' she said.

'Well, Zola, I can see you're going to make a beautiful rug.' Emily turned to Alysha. 'Really, all we'll have to do is show them how to end off nicely. I'm so encouraged.'

As they started work, the women lifted their voices in song, with beautiful harmonies soaring together effortlessly as they wove. Someone carried a clear high descant and others joined in with lower notes.

'I could listen to this all afternoon,' Alysha said. 'I wish I could record them. I wonder what they are singing about?'

'Singing that we are happy,' Zola said simply.

'That's good to hear,' Emily said. 'If everyone sang while they worked like you do, the world would be a happier place.'

Explanations

Weaving was slow, however, and after three hours Emily asked the women to stop and come back the next day. There were looks of disappointment all round, but she was adamant.

'We don't want to get on the wrong side of the Chief,' she said. 'If the women are late with the evening meal, the men will start to think that weaving is a bad idea.'

'Not once we start to sell these,' Alysha said. 'They'll probably suggest shift-work when that happens!'

She'd noticed that it was always the women who did the hard physical work around the village. Collecting wood for the fires, pounding the maize into flour, even constructing the huts from long poles and woven reeds and then covering these in handfuls of mud, was all considered 'women's work'. And the little boys herded the cattle and goats. The men appeared to do an awful lot of sitting around, although when it came to digging the wells they had been happy to do it.

She mentioned this at supper that evening.

'Traditionally, the men leave the villages to work,' Mike said. 'They go to the big cities, or work in the mines, and send money home. But there's very little employment in the cities these days.'

'Perhaps we can involve the men in selling the rugs,' Emily said. 'But first we have to produce some. I'm very pleased with what we've managed so far.'

'When's your son arriving?' Katie asked. 'Isn't it some time soon?'

'I'll be going back to Brandveld on Friday.' Emily beamed. 'Tigger's arriving that afternoon by bus. I thought we'd spend the weekend together and then he could drive me back here on Sunday evening, to start work. He's going to be ever so surprised to discover that I'm staying here, too. I haven't told him yet.'

'I'll make sure that Zukisa has his room ready for him,' Marion said. 'We've given him the big room at the back, two doors down from yours, Emily.'

Suspicions

'This is a very elastic house,' Emily remarked. 'How many rooms are there altogether?'

'Well, the original farmer had a very big family. Seven children, I believe. And then there was a sort of farm office, which is Marcus's clinic when he's here, then that little room off the *stoep*, where I think the farmer's wife used to keep an incubator for chickens. And that other room at the back which seems to have been used as a storeroom, judging by the big wooden bins we found when we arrived,' Marion said. 'Yes, luckily space is not something we're short of.'

'By the way, I thought I saw Anton Moolman's car,' Charles said. 'Parked on the hill next to the Chief's hut this afternoon. I wonder what he wanted? And why he didn't come and speak to us?'

'That's very odd,' Mike said. 'He's driven all the way down from the Orange River and he didn't pop across here for a drink before he went home? I can't think what business he has at Kliprand — it's hardly the place to plant an orange grove!'

'I think Anton does quite a lot more than just farm oranges,' Katie said quietly. 'He was talking to some rather intimidating people when we were there. Big guys in suits, hiding behind those awful wraparound sunglasses so you couldn't see their eyes. I never trust people who wear those.'

'Girl, you just don't recognise high fashion when you see it,' Alysha said. She herself seemed to have forgotten that she was connected to this same world of fashion, and happily dressed every day in a simple skirt and T-shirt.

But there's something about Alysha that just says 'special', Katie thought, looking across at her friend. She's just glowing with happiness. I hope she doesn't get a call from her agent any time soon. I'll miss her dreadfully. And so, I'm sure, will Mike.

News

Just after breakfast, Katie popped into the little office which housed the computer, the telephone and Mike's files and paperwork. These were strewn haphazardly all over the desk and didn't look as if anyone had paid them much attention lately. Administration certainly wasn't Mike's strong point!

She switched on the computer and waited while it slowly came to life.

I wish their budget would stretch to a decent, fast laptop, she thought, gazing out of the window at the cattle being driven across to the hills while the computer made various clicking noises and finally opened.

E-mails. Oh, good, one from Connor.

She opened it and immediately felt a prick of disappointment. Another short, almost impersonal note. She couldn't remember when he'd last written her a

257

long, loving letter and told her what he was really doing. He always ended with *all my love* but somehow this was starting to sound a bit hollow. On the other hand, to give him his due, he'd never been good at writing letters. She was suddenly filled with a longing to be held in his arms again and just talk, his hand in hers while they walked on the mountains above Strathcorn.

Had a great weekend again, sailing with Andrea and her father. She's a pretty neat sailor and she and her dad are entering the New England Cup next month. Came back to the city early because some of the gang were giving Rita a surprise birthday party at a club in Greenwich. Did I mention Rita before? She's the director's personal assistant and spends her spare time rock-climbing and hang-gliding. An amazing girl. You'd never say so because she's tiny and blonde and looks like a fashion plate. I got up on stage and played 'Happy Birthday' on my sax while everyone sang to her, then I stayed on with the band and we played a few numbers together. It was awesome. OK, gotta go, all my love . . .

Awesome, indeed! Since when did Connor use language like that? And where did Rita fit in, Katie wondered gloomily. The whole of New York seemed to be peopled with gorgeous, accomplished girls all vying for Connor's attention. Which he seemed perfectly willing to give them.

She clicked 'reply' and wrote crossly:

Having a great time here. Taking lots of good pictures, I think. We had an interesting meeting with the local Chief who has given his blessing to a weaving project we are setting up. This is being run by a lovely woman called Emily who lives in Brandveld but has moved in here for a while until the Namika women get going properly.

Alysha and I will help to sell the rugs once they are woven. We are all looking forward to the arrival of the vet next week.

Well, not much news. In a great

rush, lots of love.

Katie clicked 'send' before she could change her mind. She wasn't in a great rush at all. In fact, she was desperate to describe the Chief and his outfit, and the weaving they were doing, and the way the women all sang while they worked . . . but Connor's e-mail had been so brief and business-like, why should she bother?

Then she felt really mean. I'll write him a good long e-mail next time, she promised herself.

Just as she was leaving the room a 'ping' alerted her to another e-mail coming through. It was addressed to Alysha. She hoped this wasn't the e-mail from her agent calling her back to work, something that Alysha had been half expecting.

★   ★   ★

'Al!' Katie called, standing on the *stoep* and calling across to the distant schoolroom where Alysha was busy helping Emily with the weaving class. 'Mail for you!'

'I'll read it later,' Alysha shouted. Katie could tell she didn't want to read it, but she couldn't put it off for ever. Just before supper Alysha went through to the computer and stayed in there for some time. When she came out, her eyes were red.

'I've got to be in San Francisco five days from now,' she said huskily, sitting down at the table next to Mike. 'No argument. Great contract. Big bucks. I don't want to go!'

'Oh, Al, that's awful,' Katie said sympathetically. 'Can't you just refuse this assignment? Put it off for a while longer?'

'Nope. I signed a contract with my agent ages ago and I can't just cancel without any excuse. Nothing short of a broken leg would do and even then I'd have to send a doctor's certificate in triplicate.'

Mike was silent but he put his hand over hers.

'It's not the end of the world, Face. Just go over, do the shoot, and then you could come back, couldn't you? Resign, or something?'

'You don't understand, Mike,' she said shortly. 'I'm contracted for a calendar shoot in Miami straight after this and then back to France for some fashion house catalogue . . . I'm booked for the rest of this year. Even into next year! I'm stuck.'

'My goodness, Alysha, dear, I'm going to miss you!' Emily said. 'You've been a real help.'

'We'll all miss you, girlie,' Charles said. 'You just try to come back here as soon as you can.'

'I'll probably never be back,' Alysha whispered miserably. She burst into tears and left the table, slamming the bedroom door behind her.

The rest of the meal was a silent affair.

Disappointment

That night, after Katie had turned off their oil lamp, the two girls lay in the dark, listening to the sounds of the night wafting through the window. A whole family of crickets started their orchestra and somewhere a small animal squeaked and scurried. From across the valley someone called and another shouted an answer, then all was quiet.

Then Alysha cleared her throat.

'I know Mike feels something for me, I just know it,' she whispered. 'But he's never said anything. And now I'm leaving, he probably never will. So that's that.' Katie could tell she was crying.

'Al, I've seen the way he looks at you, and the way he seeks you out,' Katie said. 'Anyone can tell he's mad about you. I think he's just terribly shy when it comes to girls.'

'Maybe.' Alysha was not convinced.

'And Fran told me that he fell in love with one of the volunteers ages ago, and then she just went back to England and he never heard from her again. Perhaps he thinks you'd do the same, so he's not risking being hurt again?'

'Maybe.'

'You can write to him, Al. Send him e-mails from wherever you are, so he knows you're still thinking about him.'

'I suppose I could.'

'And he's driving you to Brandveld tomorrow, isn't he? Maybe he'll say something then.'

'Well, if he doesn't, I sure as heck won't,' Alysha said, turning over and burying her head in her pillow. 'That's the man's job. Saying something.'

Oh, dear, Katie thought, I didn't know Alysha was so old-fashioned when it came to things like this!

* * *

Early the next morning, bags packed and goodbyes said, Alysha climbed into the passenger seat next to Mike. Simba jumped up lightly and took his accustomed seat at the back, his tail wagging furiously with happiness at the thought of a trip in the Jeep.

Katie stood next to the window and gave her one last hug.

'Say something to Mike!' she whispered mischievously, but Alysha shook her head with a small smile and just stared straight ahead, biting back the tears.

As they drove off, everyone waved and Alysha turned round and fluttered her fingers forlornly at the assembled company on the *stoep*.

'She should make the flight quite easily,' Marion said, turning back to her pile of textbooks. 'She'll arrive in Cape Town at about six this evening and her flight is at ten. She can get a taxi to the airport.'

'A seven-hour bus ride and then a long flight to San Francisco? Poor girl,'

Charles said with feeling. 'I don't know how she'll manage.'

'It's worse than you think,' Katie said. 'She has to fly via London, change planes and fly to Chicago and then change again to get to California. Thirty hours of flying and goodness knows how long waiting in between. About five hours, I think.'

'I'm sorry she had to leave without any news about her cousin,' Marion remarked. 'I expect that's why she's so upset.'

Fran and Katie exchanged amused glances.

'Perhaps that's not the only reason she wanted to stay,' Fran murmured. 'But if your contacts at the church schools can come up with an address for him, Emily, we can always let her know.'

'I'm sure I'll hear something, dear,' Emily said. 'The church is a small community and someone is very likely to remember him.'

The following Sunday afternoon

everyone was sitting on the *stoep* after tea. Mike sat slightly apart from the group and appeared deep in a book, although Katie noticed he hadn't turned the pages for a long time. The other four were playing Scrabble with Marion winning, as usual.

Katie looked up at the distant sound of a motor.

'I think that must be Emily coming back. With the vet.'

Fran scrunched up her eyes and peered at the cloud of dust approaching.

'Whoever it is doesn't seem to mind the bad road.'

Soon Emily's little blue car barrelled into the yard with a squeal of brakes and a lanky blond man jumped out, walked round to the passenger door and opened it for Emily with a mock bow.

'Thank you, sweetheart,' she said. 'My goodness, I still can't get over how tall you are!'

'That would be Tigger? The overweight, Billy Bunter Tigger?' Fran whispered quietly. 'He's *gorgeous*!'

Introductions

'Wow! Well, all I can say is, if that's Tigger, he's changed for the better,' Katie murmured in amazement.

He had. A head taller than his mother, with a wiry build and an unruly thatch of blond hair, he picked up her bags together with his own and headed for the *stoep* with a long stride.

'Look, everyone, here's my son, Tigger!' Emily exclaimed happily, her arm around his waist. 'Tigs, meet everyone!'

'Hi,' he said, putting down the bags and looking around at the assembled company. 'I'm Ryan Norton, your new vet.'

A wide grin lit up his pleasant, tanned face and his brown eyes were crinkled around the edges as though he smiled a lot.

'We've been expecting you,' Marion said, shaking his hand. 'I remember you from Kenya, when you were just a little lad, Tigger — I mean, Ryan.'

'Miss Miles!' Tigger gave her a big hug. 'You haven't changed one bit. And . . . ?' He looked at Fran.

'You won't remember me,' Fran said shyly. 'I joined Help At Hand in Kenya but you'd left to study in Edinburgh the month before. Fran Moore.'

He took her hand in his, and his grip was warm and firm and his gaze direct and no-nonsense. Oh, he is nice, she thought.

'And I'm Katie Norris,' Katie said. 'A photographer.'

'And a part-time teacher, and one of my weaving assistants,' Emily added.

There was a buzz of introductions and welcomes. Fran slipped away to the kitchen and returned with a tray of glasses and a jug of cold lemon juice. Ryan Norton was certainly a pleasant surprise, and he looked as though he would fit in well and be ready for anything.

When she returned, he was deep in

conversation with Mike and Charles, his face alight with enthusiasm as he discussed his subject. He spoke slowly and authoritatively, with Katie, Marion and his mother listening with interest. Fran couldn't help noticing that Katie was watching him admiringly.

* * *

'I saw some of the Namika's cattle on our way here,' Ryan said. 'Off the top of my head I'd say it could be East Coast fever, but I'll do blood samples and check it out.'

'East Coast fever? They found a lot of that in Kenya,' Mike remarked. 'It practically destroyed the herds there in some places. But surely we're a long way from the East Coast?'

'Nope.' Ryan shook his head. 'It was first identified there, but it's a tick-borne disease and it's spread to cattle all over Africa.'

'So is there a vaccination or something to help?'

'Sure. They've actually had something for a long time but it was expensive and difficult to administer. Now they've improved the vaccine and made it a lot cheaper and easier to handle.'

'If you can do something to improve the cattle it would be a huge plus,' Mike said. 'The Namika regard their cattle as their wealth but they're a pretty bony, sorry lot. I doubt whether they get more than a few cups of milk a day from their cows.'

'Talking of bony, you've grown so thin, Tigger, sweetheart,' Emily interrupted. 'We'll need to fatten you up!'

'Spoken like a mother,' Ryan said fondly. 'Mum, what you see is me without the puppy fat and the boarding school stodge that I ate for ten years of my life. Hopefully, I'm never going to get back to the shape I was in before.'

Fran thought he looked just right, slim and energetic. She couldn't imagine him overweight.

'There's something else different I

can't put my finger on,' Emily said. 'Oh! It's your glasses! They've gone!'

'Contacts, Mum,' he said. 'I broke my glasses once too often and decided to make the change. They're much easier in hot weather.'

'Doesn't the heat get to you?' Katie asked. 'Coming from the UK, I mean. The first couple of weeks here, I really suffered. Not any more, though.'

'I love it,' Ryan said. 'But I've been studying in Pretoria for the past year so I'm pretty well acclimatised. So, tell me, what's a pretty photographer like you doing in a place like this?' His easy grin told her he was laughing at this old chestnut of a chat-up line.

Envy

Katie was still explaining what she did when Zukisa announced that supper was ready and waiting.

'Shall I — ' Fran started quietly, intending to show Ryan where he'd be sleeping, but Katie forestalled her.

'Let me show you to your room,' Katie said. 'I'm sure you'll want a wash before we eat. I'll also show you where the loo is. You won't believe it!'

'Oh, yes, I will!' Ryan laughed. 'Don't forget I was brought up on a mission station in the bush in Kenya. Our family didn't have much in the way of convenience when I was a kid. Remember the kitchen, Mum, where we had to pump water from that well outside?'

'How could I forget?' Emily said. 'It took me a long time to get used to all the luxury of being in a civilised village.'

Katie led the way down the passage

273

and when she and Ryan returned to the dining-room, Katie sat down next to him. They continued to talk animatedly about photography, while Marion ladled out servings of stew and mashed potato and the conversation at the table became general.

For someone who's supposed to be engaged to be married, she's awfully interested in our new vet, Fran thought gloomily. I think she's actually flirting with him!

She watched Katie across the table but slowly had to admit that Katie wasn't really flirting. She was just naturally friendly and treated men and women to the same cheerful banter.

A little ripple of envy washed over Fran. Girls like Katie and Alysha found it so easy to laugh and chat, while she was incredibly shy when it came to speaking to men. Especially a man as attractive as Ryan.

★   ★   ★

Connor, you'd laugh if you could see me now! I've hardly picked up my camera lately; I've been too busy helping the new vet dose the cattle with a vaccine.

He did blood tests and found they all have something called East Coast fever which is very common all through Africa. It's caused by ticks and these cattle are pretty sick. Luckily there is this new vaccine which you squirt into their mouths. The cows don't like it one little bit! But if he can cure them of this disease, the Namika people will start getting a lot more milk from their cows. Mike is going to try to find money in the budget for decent cattle feed because, as Ryan says, it's no use having healthy cows if they can't eat anything but this miserable grass.

Now how's this for a coincidence? Ryan studied at Edinburgh and knows Angus McGregor! The vet who married your cousin Audrey and I took their wedding photos, remember? He actually came to their wedding but I was *too busy to notice any of the guests. It's lovely to hear someone speak with a Scottish accent again. He makes me feel quite homesick.*

Well, this is just a short update on what's happening here. Haven't had a proper e-mail from you for ages — are you too busy or is your social life just too hectic these days?

Katie clicked *send* and sat back in her chair.

It was true. Connor's e-mails had become shorter and shorter, as though he was always in a hurry when he wrote them. She knew his working life was busy, with long hours, and his weekends were spent with his glamorous new friends, either on somebody's yacht or visiting jazz clubs in downtown New York. Perhaps writing to his girlfriend had become a chore?

But if she had to be honest, her e-mails were pretty short, too. It just seemed that her life here was so totally different from life in Strathcorn that she couldn't begin to describe it properly.

But listening to Ryan's gentle Scottish burr had made her remember her life in Strathcorn, and last night she'd been overwhelmed with sudden homesickness: for Connor, her parents, and her easy-going life in the village.

'Katie, are you up for another session of vaccinations?' Ryan asked. 'I have another fifty beauties lined up for this morning, but I'll quite understand if you're fed up with trying to persuade animals to open their mouths.'

'No, I'm fine,' Katie said. 'No stubborn bovine is going to get the better of me!' Then she looked at Fran's interested expression and added, 'How about if Fran comes along, too, as back-up? She won't take any nonsense from those cows!'

'Me? Oh, I don't know — ' Fran blushed and looked confused. 'I'm supposed to help Charles with the fencing, I think.'

'No, girlie, that's fine; I can manage without you today,' Charles said comfortably. 'You go and help Ryan and

Katie. I've got the men doing their own fencing now, anyway. I just need to take some more rolls of wire across to them.'

'Great, four hands are better than two,' Ryan said. 'OK, ladies, let's go! First we have to fetch them in from where they're grazing. Could be quite a ride.'

* * *

Ryan picked up his big veterinary bag and some sealed tins of vaccine and loaded everything into his mother's car. At the last minute, Katie picked up her camera bag and put it carefully between her knees.

'Don't know how much longer this little rattletrap will last on these roads,' he remarked as they sped off. 'But Mike's taken the Jeep and Charles needs the truck for the fencing.'

'Perhaps if you went a bit slower?' Katie's teeth were juddering from the bumps.

'Oh . . . sorry.' Ryan slowed and

negotiated the stony track down the valley, across to the village and on to the veldt beyond. 'These cattle I need to vaccinate today are grazing pretty far away from the *kraal.* So the herd boys just sleep out in the veldt with them, rather than bring them home every night. We're going to have to ask them to drive them back to the pen we built.'

'Oops, mind that tortoise!' Fran said suddenly, and Ryan swerved to a stop as a small tortoise ambled jerkily across their path.

'Sharp eyes!' he said. 'That tiny thing's the size of a coffee cup.'

'It's an African Tent,' she exclaimed, pleased. 'A baby one. See the little pointy designs on his shell, like little tents? I haven't seen one of those before, they're quite rare around here.'

'I'll take a picture,' Katie said, glad of the excuse to stop.

Namika Land

She took several photos of the little animal, which looked at her expressionlessly with small eyes, then she swung her camera on the landscape and took some more shots. By now they were several miles from the huts, and only rocky outcrops and stunted thorn trees dotted the landscape for as far as the eye could see.

Fran and Ryan got out of the car and examined the tortoise together.

'Are you keen on the wildlife around here?' Ryan asked.

'There isn't very much of it, to tell the truth,' Fran said. 'Snakes, of course. And I give those a wide berth if I can! A few tiny buck, but they're pretty rare. And hyenas, but we've never seen those; just heard them in the night.'

'And the leopard,' Katie said. 'Alysha and I definitely heard a leopard that night in the Jeep!'

'I believe you did,' Fran said. 'Although Mike wasn't convinced. Oh, look, there's some cattle.'

'Are we still on Namika land?' Katie asked. 'It's an enormous area, isn't it?'

'It's not much good to anyone, being so dry. It's practically a desert,' Ryan said grimly. 'That water you found is going to make a huge difference to the huts and vegetable gardens, of course, but there will never be enough to bring this land to life. It's useless.'

They drove up to the cattle standing listlessly cropping the tough brown clumps of grass, and greeted the two little boys herding them. They were barefoot and dressed only in brown shorts.

'These children can't be more than ten!' Katie exclaimed. 'All by themselves out here and so far from their homes.'

'They grow up tough,' Ryan said, looking in his bag and producing some sweets which were accepted gravely. 'All over Africa, they're expected to look after the cattle on their own. And woe betide them if one gets lost.'

'So how do we tell them they need to bring the cattle back home?' Katie asked. 'How's your Namika, Ryan? Mine isn't too good. In fact, it's non-existent.'

To their surprise Fran stepped forward and said something slowly and clearly, pointing towards the village.

The two boys nodded and started whistling in short, sharp bursts, clapping their hands and stirring the cattle into motion.

'Fran! I didn't know you knew any Namika!' Katie exclaimed.

'I don't, not really. Just a few words,' Fran said. 'I've been asking Zukisa for some basic sentences and I write them down in a notebook. Then I try them out with the men and they crack up laughing when I get it wrong.'

'I used to be able to speak Swahili fluently when I lived in Kenya,' Ryan said. 'But I've forgotten most of it. It's a big advantage speaking the local lingo — maybe I'll have to take lessons from you, Fran.'

She went pink.

'With pleasure.'

They stood watching the cattle move off slowly and soon there was complete silence across the veldt with only the occasional chirp of a small bird and the rustle of the wind in the long dry grass.

'What's that thumping sound?' Katie asked. The three of them strained to hear. Faintly on the breeze came a rhythmic banging, but it was too far away to tell where it came from.

★　★　★

Late that afternoon, Katie returned to the house alone, tired and sunburned. Fifty animals had been dosed for East Coast fever, many of them reluctantly, and Ryan had borne the brunt of their resistance. He was still nursing bruises to his legs where the angry cows had kicked him, and he and Fran had stopped off at the river for a swim. Katie had chosen to spend some time uploading her photographs on to the computer before supper.

'I'm exhausted!' she declared, throwing herself down on a cane chair next to Emily and Marcus, who were playing another of their intense games of Scrabble.

'Have some of Marion's lemon drink, dear,' Emily said, pouring from a glass jug that tinkled invitingly with ice cubes. 'Marcus, I am going to have to challenge that word. *Zootomy*? Never heard of it. Prepare to lose fifty points!'

'Challenge at your peril, madam!' He chuckled and watched as she thumbed her way to the end of the dictionary they kept handy.

'Oh. *The dissection of animals.* Well, all right. You win, this time!'

'I'll be kind,' he said magnanimously. 'I'll just accept a little apology for doubting my word power and I won't take off any points.'

'I don't need your charity to beat you, my good man!'

Katie downed the iced drink gratefully, then sat back and listened as Emily and Marcus sparred amiably.

Joy

It was wonderful the way Emily had fitted in with everyone at Kliprand and how she'd flourished with the company, Katie thought. Having her son here and doing something as meaningful as teaching the women to weave had made her really blossom.

Or could it be the company of Marcus? The two of them certainly got on well, sharing jokes and often sitting apart from the others and talking on the days Marcus held his clinic in the farmhouse. She'd noticed he paid little attentions to Emily: fetching her cardigan if she felt the evening breeze, or once bringing her a gift of a carved wooden donkey when he arrived from one of his far-flung clinics in the north.

'So, how did you all get on today?' Emily asked. 'And where have Ryan and Fran got to?'

'They're still at the river, swimming. And we did fine,' Katie said. 'The cattle didn't like it much but Ryan seems to have a way with animals.'

Emily smiled happily.

'He has, hasn't he? It's just so lovely having him here. Aren't I a lucky mum?'

★　★　★

Charles and Mike, Simba at his heels, returned from their day's work and joined Katie in the cane chairs. All of them stretched back and relaxed with a comfortable feeling of a day's work well done just as Fran and Ryan returned from the river.

From the huts opposite, the smoke from the evening fires started to rise as the sun slowly set, a golden backdrop to the activity of the women cooking outside.

'Who's that?' Ryan asked idly. 'A car's just driven up outside the Chief's hut.'

'That's Anton Moolman,' Mike said sharply. 'And he's got two men with him. What on earth is he doing there again? He was visiting him just the other day.'

'And he is . . . ?'

Mike filled in Ryan with the details of the generous farmer who lived along the banks of the Orange River.

'He's been pretty good to us but I wonder what his business is with the Chief? And those guys in suits look rather official.'

'There's something about him that gives me the heebie-jeebies, Mike,' Katie said. 'Something odd in his manner.'

'You've never liked him, have you?' Fran said. 'Maybe being super-wealthy makes a man a bit different.'

'I don't see how only farming oranges can make so much money,' Katie said. 'But I suppose I'm just being silly.'

'No, girlie, I don't think you are,' Charles said unexpectedly. 'I've heard a few things about Mr Moolman at the co-op over in Sandrift. The farmers there don't have much good to say about the man. He's got his fingers in a great many pies. Apparently he was involved in some rather dodgy land deal where he came off best and some small subsistence farmers were kicked off their land. He knows government officials in high places, which always helps.'

Zukisa's announcement that supper was ready signalled the end of the conversation and caused them all to forget about Anton Moolman.

Suspicions

To their surprise, soon after the meal when Marion and Fran were reading on the *stoep* by the light of an oil lamp, they heard Anton's car draw up and he got out, smiling broadly. The two men in the back of the car stayed inside, looking straight ahead.

'I was just passing, so I thought I'd bring you good people this,' he said, carrying a big carton up the steps and dropping it with a thump at their feet. 'Some grapes, picked this morning from our vines. And a nice leg of lamb. Real lamb, mind, not that goat meat that passes for food around here!'

'Goodness, Mr Moolman, how kind of you,' Marion murmured.

'Call me Anton, please. Mike not around?'

'He and Charles have just gone across to the shed to check something on the truck,' Fran said. 'They won't be long. Can we make you some coffee while you wait?'

'The shed?' he asked, ignoring her offer. 'OK, I'll find him there. Good evening, ladies.'

'I wonder what he wants?' Fran asked. 'These grapes look lovely. I'd better put the meat into the fridge. Oh, and look! He's included some bottles of wine. How nice of him.'

'He can hardly say he was just passing when he's been talking to the Chief for the past hour,' Marion said slowly. 'And those two men in the back looked as if they could be government officials. Or businessmen. They're definitely not farmers from around here. You know, the old chap is very naïve. If Mr Moolman has any dealings with him, Mr Moolman will come off best, you can be sure of that. I think Mike should ask him what's going on.'

Formalities

The following morning, Mike sent Zukisa to ask the Chief to come up to the farmhouse to see him for a discussion at his earliest convenience, and to bring Marundi with him as a translator.

'Perhaps it was nothing, but Moolman's manner last night when he came to the shed to speak to us was very odd,' Mike said.

'He didn't really have anything to say, did he?' Charles said, knocking out his pipe on the heel of his shoe. 'It was as though he was on some sort of fishing expedition. Hinting at something, definitely, but about what, I don't know! He talked in circles.'

They waited patiently for the Chief to arrive. Mike knew that to go directly to his hut wouldn't have been the correct way to do things. The old man needed time to dress correctly for a formal meeting. It was nearly an hour later when the two men came across from the little village, the Chief dressed as before, with the zebra skin cloak, but with a new headdress making him look even more magnificent than before.

Ryan had met him dressed in his usual old clothes when he talked about the cattle, but had never seen him in this attire.

'Impressive,' he murmured as Marundi and the Chief came up the steps. 'That's a lion's mane on his head, I think.'

'That's from a black-maned Kalahari lion,' Charles muttered angrily. 'They're a protected species and you only find them up in the Transfrontier Park between the Northern Cape and Botswana. I'll give you one guess who gave him that.'

'Anton Moolman,' Katie said angrily. 'I saw all his hunting rifles in his farmhouse, and his farm is pretty close to the boundaries of the Park.'

Mike greeted the Chief and they all sat down rather stiffly.

'Marundi, please ask the Chief if he can tell me what Mr Moolman wanted last night,' Mike said.

There was some muttering back and forth between them and Marundi shuffled awkwardly and said, 'My Chief is saying Mr Moolman bring him gifts. Mr Moolman knows he is an important man and he pay his respects. Which is the right thing to do.'

'Ah, so he gave the Chief that lion's mane? It's — er — very handsome,' Mike said.

Marundi translated and the Chief grinned widely and burst into animated conversation.

'My Chief tells you he also brought him a big television. For watching picture,' Marundi said.

'A television?' Marion echoed. 'But there's no electricity over at the huts! And no generators! Only the one we have here.'

'Mr Moolman, he tell the Chief he bring us electric for everyone very soon.'

'There's something very strange going on,' Mike said under his breath. Aloud he asked, 'How is Mr Moolman going to do this, Marundi? And did he say why?'

Marundi shook his head.

'He not say. But he promise very soon. He say, he come again to explain.'

And that was all they could learn on the subject.

★ ★ ★

When they'd left, Fran spoke diffidently.

'I think I heard the Chief mention a paper and writing his name on it. But he spoke so quickly, I couldn't really pick up any more.'

'I get the feeling Anton's about to cheat the Chief out of something,' Marion said suddenly. 'I read about this happening in Zambia once. Some clever mining company got the illiterate locals to sign a paper giving them the right to mine minerals on their land

and they made a fortune without paying the tribe a penny. I wonder if he could be thinking of something like that? What if there are minerals and he knows about them?'

'I don't think there could be any minerals on the Namika land,' Mike said. 'And I really don't think the man could be so underhand. He's been very generous to us, sponsoring the pumps and so on. I'm sure there'll be some rational explanation. I'll ask him when we see him again.'

'Wish Us Luck!'

'Hey, what's this? A brand new laptop?' Katie spotted the smart little machine next to the big computer in the office.

'Yes. I thought I'd better get a new one for — um — office use. That old one of ours is pretty slow.' Mike looked a bit uncomfortable. 'I thought I'd keep it separate, so it doesn't get any viruses or anything.'

'Mmm. Good idea,' Katie said, noticing with amusement that it had a perfectly good virus protector already loaded. She had a pretty good idea why Mike felt the need for a new laptop. He'd been receiving regular e-mails from Alysha and, although neither Katie nor Fran would have dreamed of reading them, perhaps he wanted to keep them completely private.

'OK, Mike, I just came to tell you that the Jeep is loaded with rugs, and

Fran and I are off to try to sell them. Zola's coming along, too. Wish us luck!'

'I do. But don't be too disappointed if you don't sell any the first time you try.'

'We'll be very disappointed if we don't sell at least five,' Katie said firmly. 'Positive thought counts a lot. And they are so cheerful, people won't be able to resist!'

It was true. The rugs the women had made were a kaleidoscope of colours — bright reds and blues and greens — some with stripes and some with diamond patterns. Emily had been very pleased with the results of just a few weeks' work and she had high hopes for the women's weaving turning into cash for them.

'Be prepared to bargain a little, but don't give them away for ridiculous prices,' she said. 'I know the fabric didn't cost us anything but the women have worked long and hard on these. Use your discretion when it comes to prices.'

'We will,' Fran promised.

They bumped along the road to Brandveld in high spirits. Zola, one of the women who had turned out to be an excellent weaver, was grinning from ear to ear in the back, humming to herself.

'Just imagine if we sell a lot,' Fran said. 'The women would be earning money for the first time in their lives! I wonder what they'll do with it?'

'Buy a cow, I expect,' Katie said. 'That seems to be their idea of true wealth.'

'No, I think they'd send their children to a proper boarding school,' Fran said. 'They are all so pleased with Marion's education I know they'd love their kids to carry on to high school. But so far, no Namika child has ever been higher than grade six.'

'Except Alysha's grandfather, Tulema Mabenda,' Katie said. 'And he went on to be a doctor in London. It just shows you what people can do if they get the chance.'

When they reached Brandveld, they parked in the shade of a thorn tree on the side of the tarred road, and unpacked the rugs.

Zola spread them out on the Jeep until the vehicle looked like a brightly covered mound of stripes.

Then all three stood next to the Jeep, waiting hopefully. And waited and waited.

Over the next two hours, several cars flashed past, but they didn't slow down at all. The wind from their passing dislodged the rugs and made them slide to the ground.

'Honestly! You'd think they'd at least be interested enough to stop and ask what we're doing here,' Katie said. 'I'm going across to the shop for some drinks.'

She returned with three cold sodas and Lettie in tow, who was fascinated by the rugs.

'These are so cool! They're beautiful!' she exclaimed. 'Did Mrs Burroughs teach them how to do these?'

'Yes, they are nice, aren't they? But no-one wants to stop and look,' Fran said. 'At this rate we'll be lucky if we sell even one.'

Lettie went back to the shop and left the three of them staring off into the distance as a car appeared on the horizon. To their amazement, Zola rushed out into the middle of the road, energetically waving a rug like a giant flag. For a moment it looked as though the driver would simply swerve around her, but the car braked to a stop and backed up.

A woman opened the door and walked back to them.

'We sell!' Zola whispered happily.

'And what are these?' the woman asked. She was tall and slim and dressed as though she were going to a business meeting. Dark glasses hid her eyes, but she sounded interested.

Katie explained where the rugs came from and how they were made, and the woman fingered the rugs critically, then turned them over and checked the finishing at the back.

'Nice,' she said. 'African primitive. They have a certain charm. I like them. How much?'

Oh, heavens, Katie thought frantically, looking at Fran. We forgot to decide how much we'd ask! But the woman looked as though she could spare a few pennies. She drove a big imported saloon car and had the indefinable look that spelled money and success.

'Two hundred rand?' Katie ventured.

They could always bargain, she decided. If Fran agreed, they could go as low as fifty rand if it meant they'd make just one sale.

'And how many have you here?'

'Um . . . ' Fran counted quickly. 'Thirty-five.'

'Right. I'll take the lot. Can I give you a cheque?'

Katie swallowed hard.

'Sure,' she croaked. 'I think we could do that, don't you, Fran?'

Fran cleared her throat.

'A cheque would be fine, I guess. Do you have a shop?'

'Interior design, sweetie,' the woman said. 'Here's my card. Call me Phyllis.'

Phyllis Greenway Interiors, Hout Street, Cape Town was printed in gold on a shiny black surface alongside two phone numbers as well as her e-mail address.

'You might have seen my work in the latest 'Home And Pleasure'? Or the four page spread they gave me in 'Society'?'

'Not yet,' Katie murmured.

'And what are your names, sweeties?' Phyllis signed her cheque with a flourish and gave it to Katie. Seven thousand rand! Katie thought she might faint.

'Katie Norris and Fran Moore. And this is Zola Mintendi.'

'Hi, there. I tell you what, I'd love to get a shot of the three of you. And a head shot of Zola. Zola, are you one of the weavers on this project?'

Zola nodded happily, not entirely sure what Phyllis had asked.

Doubts

The three of them stood self-consciously smiling at the camera in front of the rugs. Katie couldn't help noticing that Phyllis held her little digital slightly crooked, and that she'd have taken a better picture if they weren't all looking into the sun, but she said nothing. They set about folding up the rugs and loading them into the capacious boot of Phyllis's saloon.

'I'd like your phone number, please,' Phyllis said, proferring a leather-covered notebook. 'And your e-mail address, if you have one? I might want to repeat my order if these do well. Which I think they will.'

Fran wrote the information in her book and Phyllis neatly folded herself into her car and drove off, waving cheerily as she did so.

The three watched her silently.

'Well!' Katie said finally, unable to believe the amount on the cheque she was holding. 'Never in my wildest dreams did I expect a stroke of luck like that!'

'She pay us money?' Zola asked anxiously.

'Yes, she did,' Katie said. 'But we have to send it to the bank first, before we can get it.'

Zola looked blank.

'Marundi will explain when we get home,' Katie said brightly. 'We'll have the money later. Lots of it.'

'Katie,' Fran said slowly. 'I hate to say it, but we could have been taken for a very convincing ride. We don't really know anything about that woman. What if Phyllis Greenway's cheque bounces?'

Sales Ladies

'You think Phyllis Greenway's cheque might *bounce*?' Katie went cold all over. Fran was right, of course. What an idiot she'd been! Accepting a cheque from a total stranger just because she flashed a smart business card. If the cheque wasn't honoured, this could mean weeks of work thrown away and all the Namika women who'd worked so hard would have their hopes dashed.

As it was, they were hoping she and Fran would return with a few rugs sold and real folding money to show for it. The concept of a cheque, even if it proved to be a good one, was not easy to explain and certainly wouldn't look like any sort of money to the women of the tribe.

'No, I'm not saying I think it will bounce. I'm just saying it might,' Fran said. 'But if it does, it's not your fault. I liked the look of Phyllis Greenway as much as you did, and besides, we have her business address and we can always find her. Let's buy some cold drinks for us all to celebrate our fabulous success as sales ladies!'

Yeah, right, positive thinking, Katie thought. Just what I told Mike I had. So why do I have this sinking feeling inside?

But the sight of Zola enjoying her first ice-cold drink cheered her up enormously and she turned the Jeep towards home feeling upbeat again.

They'd hardly driven a mile when a cloud of dust signalled another vehicle coming towards them at speed, and Ryan, driving his mother's car, skidded to a halt next to them.

'What's wrong?' Katie called in alarm. 'Has something happened at Kliprand?'

Ryan climbed out and grinned a bit sheepishly.

'I was worried about you girls,' he said. 'I didn't like the idea of you standing on the side of the road accosting strangers. When Mike told me you'd all gone off on your own, I thought I'd better come and — well, give you some back-up if you needed it. I'm glad you're all right.'

Katie couldn't help noticing he was looking at Fran as he spoke.

'You daft man!' Fran said. 'We're perfectly able to look after ourselves. But it was very nice of you to think of us.'

'So — you're coming back a lot earlier than we thought. How did you do?'

'Sold out!' Katie said. It was very satisfying to see Ryan's incredulous expression. She only hoped it was true.

'Are you going to follow us back?' she asked, putting the Jeep into gear.

'Yep, I guess so,' Ryan said. 'Um, tell you what, Fran, why don't you keep me company? I don't like to drive all the way on my own. Maybe you can teach me a few more words of Namika?'

'All right,' Fran said, climbing out

with alacrity. She grinned shyly at Katie as she closed the passenger door and Katie got the feeling that they wouldn't be speaking too much Namika on the way home.

Well, she was just going have to practise some herself, with Zola!

Old Africa Hands

'Fran, are you very busy, or do you fancy a trip to Upington? I need to collect some veterinary supplies,' Ryan said.

It was a few days later, and Charles and Fran were looking at some rough plans to build Ryan a clinic of his own. It would be more of a storeroom than a clinic, because all the animals he dealt with were out in the field, and he doubted that anyone around Kliprand would ever bring in a furry pet.

'I'm not sure — Charles, are we going to start on this today?'

'I'd like to get the foundations dug, but that's not your concern,' Charles replied cheerfully. 'I'll get three of the men to give me a hand. You go on with Ryan. You've never been to Upington, have you?'

'Not yet. OK, I'll come along for the ride.'

Ryan had commandeered the Jeep for the trip and they set off about an hour later. Their route took them through Brandveld and up north, thankfully on a tarred road.

'What a pleasure to be able to hear yourself speak!' Fran remarked. 'I'd forgotten what a luxury a smooth road can be.'

'So, you've been with Help At Hand for how long? Five years?' Ryan looked at her. 'I can't imagine you'd want to end up here?'

Fran smiled.

'I haven't ended up. This is just — I don't know — a chapter in my life, I think. I don't see myself staying with Mike and the others for ever. My father would like me back home to get involved with his business, but I've learned one thing from being here: Africa gets into your blood. I don't know if I could go back and live in Canada ever again. But I haven't decided.'

'You're right about Africa getting to

you,' Ryan said thoughtfully. 'When I was at school in Kenya I always imagined I'd study in Scotland and work there once I'd qualified. It seemed so romantic. But, even with a good job in Dundee, I couldn't wait to come back here. And although I've never been to this part of Africa, it felt like coming home.'

'This is very different from Kenya, though.'

'I know, it's so unbelievably harsh and dry. Actually, once I've got my six months' experience in Kliprand, what I'd really like to do is go back to Kenya and run my own veterinary service. Not in a big town, but somewhere in the high lands. The livestock belonging to the tribesmen have a very high mortality level and they could do with some help.'

'I really loved Kenya,' Fran said. 'I've worked in three African countries with Help At Hand and that was the best posting of all. I didn't mind the hard life out in the bush because the people were so friendly there.'

'Really?' He grinned. 'I can see the two of us turning into those leathery sunburned folk that people describe as Old Africa Hands.'

She grinned.

'Like Marcus?'

'He's a really good guy. I wouldn't mind being like Marcus when I grow old. He just seems completely happy with who he is, and what he does with his life.'

'You're right, he's a lovely man. He and your mum get on pretty well, don't they?'

'Yes, I've noticed that.' Ryan paused. 'Mum's had a pretty hard life, I think. My father wasn't a very easy man to live with and now she's all on her own in Brandveld, and that's such a tiny backwater of a place. I could tell from her letters that she was lonely, so it's great that she's met up with all of you again. And I think Marcus is good for her — he's the first man I've seen who can beat her at chess!'

The road stretched ahead, straight and flat. Beyond the wire fencing on either side, a few thin cattle could be seen every now and then, cropping at the brown, dry grass with only intermittent clumps of thorn trees adding a touch of tired green to the landscape.

As they neared Upington the countryside became noticeably greener with crops of some sort covering the flat farmlands.

'Once you have water, you can grow anything up here,' Ryan said. 'The farmers irrigate from the Orange River and do very well.'

'Like Anton Moolman,' Fran replied. 'His place is wonderfully green and lush. He's right on the river, too.'

Upington was a small town on the edge of the Orange River with wide streets edged with single-storey shops. Well-tended trees and immaculate green lawns in front of the public buildings made it different from anything Fran had seen for months, and the whole place was buzzing with activity. An unusually large number of farm trucks lined the main road through the centre.

'It's Friday,' Fran recalled. 'All the farm workers are in town to spend their wages. We'll be lucky to find parking anywhere.'

'I have the address of the suppliers. Maybe they'll have a spot for us.'

Ryan was right. The veterinary suppliers had a big car park at the back of their building and Fran waited in the shade while Ryan went inside to collect his order. He was back within minutes and loaded the boxes in the back.

'OK, I have an idea.' He grinned. 'Have you ever been to the Augrabies Falls?'

'Never,' Fran said. 'But I've heard they're spectacular.'

'And they're just over an hour's drive from here.' Ryan slammed the door. 'What d'you say to lunch at the Falls?'

'I say that's a great idea. This is turning into a real day off!'

'Another World'

As they followed the road along the river, it became wider and flowed faster, although the water was brown and didn't look very inviting. Palm trees grew abundantly with great bunches of golden dates hanging below, and vineyards with dark purple grapes marched in neat rows over the horizon.

'This is another world from Kliprand, isn't it?' Fran murmured. 'I wish I could take all this greenery back in a bottle and share it with everyone!'

'Well, we can take something back,' Ryan said. 'These farm stalls along the road sell fresh dates. And bunches of grapes. And look at the oranges, they're enormous! We'll stock up on the way back after lunch.'

They drove through the big gates of the national park and found a spot in the shade opposite the restaurant.

'I'm famished,' Ryan said. 'Let's — '

'Ryan, listen! Is that the roar of the Falls? We simply must go and look first, just for a minute.'

'They're called Augrabies because that means Place of Great Noise, in the Khoi language,' Ryan told her, quoting from a pamphlet they'd been handed at the gate. 'Well named.'

A stony path leading towards the river gave way to enormous smooth rocks and the noise of the falling water became louder as they approached it. As the Falls came into sight it was almost deafening. The two of them stood on the biggest of the rocks near the edge and gazed without speaking at the torrent of brown water shooting over the edge with such force that it turned into a creamy foam, then thundered down a hundred feet into a whirling chasm below. Fran was so awestruck by this explosion of nature's power that she found herself trembling and instinctively reached for Ryan's hand. He embraced her, warm and secure in his arms.

'Amazing,' he whispered.

'Terrifying,' Fran said. 'Let's go and have lunch!'

They held hands all the way back to the restaurant.

An Award For Marcus

'Shouldn't Tigger and Fran be back by now?' Emily fretted, looking at her watch. 'It's eight o'clock and they've missed supper.'

'Relax, Em,' Marcus said. 'They've probably stopped for a meal on the way back, somewhere like Kakamas. There's a nice little restaurant there.'

'I wish he'd phone, though. Aha . . . I believe you're in check!' Emily slid her bishop across the board and sat back, triumphant.

'That's a very sneaky move.' As Marcus studied the board ruefully, the phone rang inside the house. They heard Marion answering, and after a short conversation she came out to the *stoep*.

'That was Fran, to tell us she and Ryan won't be home tonight,' she said. 'They went to the Augrabies Falls for lunch and when they wanted to leave they found they had a flat tyre. And then they discovered the spare was missing.'

'Oh, heck.' Mike looked guilty. 'My fault. I took it across to the workshop to mend the puncture and haven't got round to it yet.'

'So now they're sitting there waiting, because tomorrow's Sunday and there are no service garages open until Monday morning.'

'My goodness.' Emily looked upset. 'Poor Fran. I mean, she didn't go prepared for an overnight stay . . . And where will they sleep? In the Jeep?'

'Of course not,' Marion said. 'They've taken chalets in the National Park and there's a perfectly good shop there. I'm sure she can buy whatever she needs. And I have to say Fran sounded very cheerful!'

'Lucky things!' Katie said. 'I've always wanted to go up to the Falls. I've heard they're wonderful.'

'A weekend at the Falls sounds pretty

good to me, too,' Mike agreed. 'I think we all need a break every now and then. By the way, Marcus, are you going down to Cape Town to receive that award? Planning a few days down at the coast?'

'Me? Not at all,' Marcus said shortly. He looked uncomfortable. 'Load of nonsense.'

'Marcus, how can you say that? The Provincial Medal of Honour?' Marion sounded quite upset. 'They don't give that to just anybody, you know! It's a real recognition of the work you've been doing all these years.'

'The work I do is what I want to do,' he said. 'Awards don't mean a thing. They've invited me to a black tie evening ceremony and they want to give me a medal. Now, if they gave me some money to build a proper maternity clinic around here, that would be worth something.'

'Blame My Father'

'Why did you come all the way up to the Northern Cape in the first place, Marcus?' Katie had often wondered why a doctor of his obvious ability would settle himself so far from every modern medical facility. 'Don't you sometimes wish you were attached to some big hospital with all the equipment you need?'

'Blame my father,' Marcus said with a wry smile. 'He was a heart specialist and a very wealthy man. Actually, he was a good doctor and his patients came from all over the country to consult him, and, of course, I hero-worshipped him when I was a kid. I never wanted to be anything else but a doctor, like he was. But once I'd graduated I realised that he and I had very different ideas of what this meant. I had this idealistic notion that we were intended to help people, but he kept talking about the money I could make.'

'Some fathers do tend to think along those lines,' Charles said dryly. 'Especially if their son has just spent seven expensive years at university.'

'Maybe you're right. But he wanted me to study longer and become a specialist — in anything, just so I could set up on my own in some fancy consulting rooms. So to show him what I thought of his idea, I went off to the Transkei, to a part they call the Wild Coast, and worked in a small rural hospital there. In those days, the conditions were very rough and ready, and the pay was pitiful, but I was hooked.'

Emily patted his hand.

'You do wonderful work here, Marcus, and there are so many people who are thankful you didn't listen to your father! But I still wish you'd go and accept that award. It seems quite rude just to ignore it.'

'Cape Town's a long way to go just

for a glass of wine and a boring speech,' he said. 'Mind you, if I had company . . .' He looked at Emily hesitantly. 'Would you like to drive down with me? Just for the kind of break Mike was talking about?'

'Oh, I'd love to!' Emily beamed. 'I could visit that factory that sends us the rags for the weaving, couldn't I?'

'And you could call on Phyllis Greenway's shop and see how our rugs are selling there. Her cheque cleared, thank heavens, so maybe she'd like to order some more.'

'And I could give you a shopping list if you'll be anywhere near a good supermarket,' Marion said.

'Oh, if you're passing the industrial area, maybe you could pop in to that plumbers' warehouse and see if they've got those plastic pipes we've been waiting for. If you went down by truck, you could just stack them in the back . . .' Mike looked hopeful.

'And we could even pick up that daft medal if we have time.' Marcus grinned. 'OK, ladies and gentlemen, place your orders. Emily and I will leave for Cape Town on Monday. But we definitely won't be driving that truck!'

Interesting News

On Sunday evening Mike opened his laptop and checked his e-mails, something he did every evening before joining the others for supper.

His daily letter from Alysha was waiting for him and he opened it with a smile of expectation. Sometimes she just sent a few lines, or only a joke, but sometimes she wrote at great length. Tonight her letter was full of excited exclamation marks.

Darling Mike, I have so much news, I don't know where to start!

All right: big news number one! I have found my long-lost cousin Bona Mabenda and contacted him. Katie sent me his e-mail address, which Emily got from the Bishop — and he's already written back to me.

He's pretty high up in the government service, a sort of under-minister working in something called the Energy Department. I can't imagine what that is — perhaps electricity? But he sounds very nice. I told him I'd been in Kliprand and all about the work your guys are doing there, and he says he's always wanted to visit again but just never had the time.

So, then: big news number two. In three weeks' time I'm coming back, for about a week, or maybe longer — it depends on what my agent has lined up for me. Happy? I am! And Bona is going to come down and meet me and all of you, of course. He's very interested in what Help At Hand is doing.

Big news number three: remember those stones I picked up, with pretty green streaks? I took them back as keepsakes and one of the other models who was rooming with me in Paris showed them to her boyfriend who works in the geology department at the university there, and he reckons they have traces of malachite in them, which *could mean there is copper underground at Kliprand. How about that?! Start digging!*

When I've finished here, I've got a three-day shoot in New York and from there we go back to Florida for a week — but I'll be arriving September 3 at Brandveld. I hope you can tear yourself away to come and meet the bus. All my love, Alysha.

Mike sat for a moment, his whole being flooded with happiness at Alysha's news. She was coming back. And this time, he was going to make very sure she didn't leave again.

A Discovery

When Mike thought of seeing Alysha, the news in the rest of her letter hardly seemed significant. But he read the letter once again, then selected a small portion of it and printed it out for the others to read at the supper table.

'Have a look at this,' he said. 'You remember those pretty green stones Alysha found? A geologist in Paris told her they have traces of malachite in them and that's usually a sign of copper below ground.'

'Are you seriously thinking the Namika could be sitting on a potential copper mine?' Charles said. 'This could make a huge difference to them.'

'If it were true, you'd be right. But what are the chances of finding copper here? Probably one in a thousand. And they'd need a lot of capital just to do a bit of exploration underground. We wouldn't be able to help them — we're not miners.'

'Couldn't we ask some mining company to take a look? Then if they found copper, we could at least help the Namika people work out some sort of deal where they could get a percentage of the profits.'

'That's one possibility. But I'd like to show some of these stones to a mining chap in Upington first, just to see what he thinks. No point in getting excited until we're sure,' Mike said. 'Although we know there's an old copper mine on the other side of Sanddrift but that was mined out years ago. There's nothing there now, it's like a ghost town.'

'You know that banging sound we've all heard lately?' Katie said slowly. 'What if that is someone looking for copper?'

Mike shook his head.

'Who would that be? There's no-one here but the Namika people and they don't know anything about mining.'

'No, but Anton Moolman might.

What if he also spotted those stones when he visited here and realised what they could mean? And he's been around talking to the Chief recently, hasn't he?'

Mike was silent.

'That's possible, I suppose. Last time he came over he was hinting at something he was interested in, but never told me straight out. And I can't see Anton doing anything with the Namika without talking to us first. He knows we're here to help them find ways to make a living. And besides, he's a farmer, not a mining magnate!'

'He has government contacts, though,' Charles put in. 'He's a man of many interests, as he said. And I'm sure he'd love to get involved with copper. Anyone with a copper mine would make a fortune.'

'I'll ask him about it when we see him again,' Mike said comfortably. 'There's no rush.'

* * *

But, to everyone's surprise, a few mornings later, Marundi and the Chief appeared without warning on the *stoep* just after breakfast.

Marundi was dressed for a formal occasion in his suit and well-polished shoes, but the Chief wore only his usual clothes with his headdress of the lion's black mane adding the note of authority.

'We talk,' he said sternly.

'Please, sit down, Chief,' Mike invited.

The old man took a chair with Marundi standing next to him ready to act as interpreter.

'What can we do for you?' Mike asked uncertainly.

The Chief stared stonily at him and said something in Namika. Marundi spoke softly.

'The Chief say, you must leave our land.'

'What?' Mike was stunned and everyone looked shocked. 'Why does he say this?'

There was more conversation between them, then Marundi said almost apologetically, 'Chief say, Mr Moolman tell us he give us electricity. But Mr Moolman, he say you must go. Everyone must go. Now.'

Mike was stunned.

'Marundi, what nonsense is this? Mr Moolman doesn't own this land! This all belongs to you, the Namika people, and he's got no say here about what you do or don't do.'

Marundi shuffled uncomfortably and looked at his feet.

'Does your chief really want Help At Hand to go, Marundi? Doesn't he want your children to go to school? Doesn't he want the women to make the rugs and sell them? Isn't he pleased with the water pipes and taps so you can grow vegetables?'

'No, Mr Mike, is Mr Moolman say you must go, not the Chief. Look, Mr Mike, here is the paper he gave us.' He produced a sheet of paper and put it on the table.

Mike scanned it quickly, then sat down to read it more fully.

'Look at this,' he said angrily, passing it to the others. 'It's a contract Anton's drawn up for the old man to sign. He's offering to lay on electricity for all the huts in the village, but only once he's got a copper mine up and running!'

'So he *did* know something,' Katie said. 'That banging we heard must have been his men chiselling off chunks of rock. Then he must have sent them away to be analysed, so he's definitely found enough evidence to make it worth his while to start mining.'

'Now he's trying to get the Chief to sign away all rights to their land. No wonder he wants us away from here. It says, *All foreign aid groups to be banned from entering the Namika tribal territory within four weeks of the signing of this contract.*'

'And he's planning to strip mine, by the looks of it,' Charles growled. 'See here, he says he wants complete control of an area not less than twenty

334

thousand acres — that's huge!'

'And we all know what strip mining does,' Marion said. 'Remember Mali, when they destroyed that entire ancient settlement and poisoned all the water, mining for some obscure mineral needed for space capsules?'

'I don't suppose the Chief has any idea of what he's signing away,' Mike said. 'He's probably never heard of strip mining. It would be a complete disaster here.'

He turned to Marundi.

'Marundi, please tell the Chief this is not a good paper to sign. It's a very bad paper. Tell him the Namika people will lose all their land for their cattle. Mr Moolman will scrape away all the soil so you won't be able to grow food. The air will be dirty with dust and your children will get chest problems. The water in the river will become poisoned. He really must not sign this contract.'

The two muttered together, then Marundi said, 'Mr Moolman he say, big jobs for everyone. Earn lots of money.

You must leave here, no arguments please.'

But he looked so unhappy and embarrassed when he translated the pronouncement of his Chief that Mike felt sorry for him.

The Chief was a traditional tribal man who had never been out of the area and was easily convinced by a smooth talker like Anton Moolman, but Marundi had worked in a city for years and probably knew the ways of the world a lot better.

'Marundi, listen to me. Ask the Chief not to write his name on this paper until I have spoken to an important government man in Pretoria who can do something better for all the Namika people. Ask him to give me a week to do this.'

Mike stared intently at the Chief while Marundi spoke.

The Chief was silent, chewing his lip, then he muttered something heavily.

'One week only,' Marundi said. He gave Mike a small apologetic smile as the two of them left the *stoep*.

'An important government man?' Marion asked in disbelief. 'You don't know anyone like that!'

'Maybe not. But Alysha does,' Mike said. 'And sometimes it's who you know that counts.'

As he headed back to his computer to write to Alysha, he just hoped her cousin Bona Mabenda was as important as she thought he was.

Alone

Marcus and Emily drove off in Marcus's battered old Jeep first thing on Monday morning but it was late afternoon before Fran and Ryan came back to Kliprand. Ryan drove the Jeep to park it in the shade of the gum tree and Fran came up the stairs into the house.

She dumped a big carton of fruit on the table in the dining-room.

'Look, oranges we picked ourselves!' she said. 'And these dates came from date palms just growing on the side of the road.'

Katie was uploading her latest photographs on to the computer.

'Never mind the fruit! A weekend with Ryan? How was it?'

Fran flushed.

'It was fantastic. The Falls are unbelievable. And the animals were everywhere — we saw buck, zebras and giraffes, and the most enormous tortoises.'

'Hi, Katie,' Ryan said, coming up behind Fran. 'Has Fran been telling you about our amazing weekend? The Falls were stunning. I just wish we'd had a camera with us. Katie, you have to go up and see for yourself. You could get some wonderful shots for your book.'

'The Falls are hardly part of the Help At Hand work! But I'd love to go one day, before I leave.'

But not by myself, she thought. I wish Connor were here, I'd love to go up to the Falls with him. I'd love him to see all this space and emptiness and just understand everything I've been looking at for all these months.

She was overwhelmed suddenly with a feeling of being all alone. Fran and Ryan seemed to have formed a close friendship. Mike had Alysha arriving soon, even though she'd probably be off again after a week or two. And Emily and Marcus were away together, obviously pleased with each other's company.

It's time I went home to Scotland, Katie thought. And I want Connor to be there, too.

Worry

'Mike, have you heard from Alysha since you told her about Anton Moolman's mining scheme?'

Katie was on her way back to the house after taking shots of some children playing with some baby goats. She'd been fascinated by how amiable the pure white babies were, leaping about with the children and providing so many photo opportunities, but how bad-tempered their mothers were.

After a run-in with a belligerent goat where she'd come off worst, Katie had dusted off her rear end and given the adults a wide berth.

Mike paused from his task of off-loading cans of diesel next to the shed.

'Not a word,' he said. 'I'm a bit worried, actually. I expected her to reply as soon as she read my e-mail but there's been dead silence. I don't know if she even received it. And she'll be here in four days.'

'And aren't you a happy man!' Katie teased. 'Would you like Fran and me to go across to Brandveld and meet the bus?'

'Um — no, thanks. It's quite all right, I'm willing to go. There'll be mail to collect, as well, and lots of supplies from the shop.'

Katie laughed out loud.

'As if we would!' she said. 'We all know wild horses wouldn't keep you from meeting her! And Alysha would be livid to see anyone else tagging along. She'll want you all to herself for a little while.'

He grinned broadly but said nothing. Katie could see he was still a bit unwilling to tell everyone how far things had developed between him and the gorgeous model.

Ever since Alysha had left Kliprand to return to work in Europe, she'd been in almost daily contact with Mike through e-mails. But Mike wasn't the only one she wrote to. Alysha had written ecstatic e-mails to Katie, telling her exactly how she felt, and if the two of them didn't announce their engagement while she was here, Katie would be very surprised.

She and Mike walked back to the house together.

'We're getting pretty close to the Chief's deadline,' Katie said. 'I don't think he really wants us to leave at all, but Anton is such a forceful kind of man. And all those promises he dangles in front of the Chief . . . '

'And they're only promises. Once he's signed away the Namika land to Moolman he can whistle for the electricity and everything else he thinks they'll be given.' Mike scowled. 'But we'll work something out, I'm sure. It's a pity we can't contact Alysha's cousin directly and see if he can do something.'

'It's probably better that she asks him,' Katie said. 'She's his relative and the Namika are very strong on family. I just wish we knew if she's already written to him and if he's planning to help.'

★ ★ ★

It was that magic time of day at Kliprand, when the sun had set and the brilliant blue of the sky had turned to a glow of orange and yellow, before sinking further into the deep blues of twilight. Everyone was sitting on the *stoep* just watching this silent extravaganza of colour when a familiar car barrelled noisily down the track to the huts across the valley.

'That's Anton Moolman,' Charles said gloomily. 'Come to collect his bit of paper, I suppose.'

'He's no business coming back here already,' Marion said angrily. 'The Chief gave Mike a week to speak to Alysha's cousin.'

'He probably doesn't know that,' Ryan said. 'He thinks he just has to get the Chief's signature and he can start doing as he wants.'

'Right,' Mike said, standing up abruptly. 'I'm going across to speak to Moolman directly. He's been avoiding us because he knows what he's proposing is actually a way to cheat the Namika out of their mineral rights. Coming, Charles? Ryan?'

'Men only?' Marion queried tartly. 'I don't think so, Mike. This affects all of us. Come on, girls.'

Unwelcome Visitor

Katie automatically scooped up her camera and the six of them walked single file down the rutted path and up to the huts. Smoke rose from fires in the twilight and the women stirring the food stood up and welcomed them with shy smiles.

The Chief's hut was larger than the others, surrounded by a rough hedge of dried thorn bushes which made an effective boundary for the chickens and pigs in the yard, with a lopsided gate leaning across the opening. When the Chief saw the group heading towards him, he shouted something and a small boy ran out and moved the gate aside to let them pass.

Anton Moolman and the Chief were sitting on plastic chairs and the ever-present Marundi stood behind them. The two Namika men were smoking, obviously enjoying the luxury of cigarettes from an opened wholesale carton of packets Anton had brought as a gift.

'Good evening to you, Chief.' Mike walked up and shook his hand, nodding to the other man as he did so. 'Evening, Anton.'

Anton grunted and looked at him narrowly without speaking, while the others respectfully shook the Chief's hand using the traditional African handshake which included twisting the thumb. This had taken some practice when she first arrived, but Katie was pleased to see she had perfected it, smoothly sliding her hand up to grasp his thumb before gripping and shaking his palm again.

Almost immediately the Chief's children brought out small wooden stools and the party sat down, all facing him.

'Your pigs are looking very healthy,' Mike said, with Marundi translating. 'And I see you have many more chickens since I last visited.'

Decision

His wife probably handed over her share of the rug money, Katie thought. Fair enough, chickens and eggs are just what they need.

'My pigs are good and fat,' the Chief agreed. 'And my chickens are multiplying.'

'And your children are growing strong and healthy,' Mike continued, knowing that no business could be discussed without the correct conversational preliminaries.

'My children are growing tall, yes.'

Katie was aware of the women all straining to hear, although they had stayed where they were next to the fires. Of course, they'd know why Anton Moolman was visiting and what he wanted. They knew that if he had his way, and Help At Hand had to leave, the little school would close and there'd be no more water taps installed or help for their animals.

'Say what you've come to say, Mike,' Anton barked. 'I know you're here about the mine. But it's a done deal, my friend.'

Mike ignored him and spoke to the Chief.

'Sir, have you already written your name on Mr Moolman's paper? The week you gave us is not yet over, as I'm sure you know.'

Marundi translated somberly and the Chief looked at Mike and then at Anton.

'I have not yet written my name. But I am going to.'

'Aha! You hear that, Mike? The Chief's made his decision like a sensible man.' Anton was gloating.

'I am going to write my name in four days' time,' the Chief continued. 'Not tonight. I said I would wait for seven days and I am a man of my word.'

'Come on, Chief, use your brains,' Anton said irritably. 'Think of the benefits you'll all have once the mine is up and running. Work for your men, money in your pocket . . . '

'These men aren't miners,' Mike said quietly. 'You'll be bringing in outsiders to operate your machines and your proposed strip-mine will destroy the Namika land. And as we both know, any money that comes from the copper will go straight into your own pocket.'

'Don't talk rubbish!' Anton's face purpled with rage. 'My friend the Chief and I have an agreement and he's going to stick to it. Because he's a man of honour, right, Chief?'

'Moolman's making a big mistake,' Marion murmured to Katie. 'He's not respecting the Chief, shouting at him like that.'

'This land belongs to the Namika and if the Chief wants to see a mine here, that's his right!' Anton continued aggressively.

'I agree. It's their land and they can do what they like with it,' Mike said. 'But the Chief is not a sophisticated man and doesn't realise what his signature will mean. It will give you a free hand to pollute their water and spoil their grazing lands for ever.'

'That's nonsense. Anyway, their cattle are a scrawny, sorry lot. Not worth keeping.'

Hostility

Marundi murmured to the Chief who narrowed his eyes and turned his stony gaze to Anton.

'Their cattle represent the traditional wealth of these people,' Mike said levelly. 'They might not look like prize-winners but they're healthier now that our vet has taken care of them.'

'If you think I'd let a few miserable cattle stand in the way of a mining development, you're crazy,' Anton said.

'There are many ways to develop a mine, but strip-mining is the cheapest and the most destructive to this land and the environment,' Mike snapped.

'And your demand that the Chief tells everyone from Help At Hand to leave here is ridiculous,' Marion broke in. 'We've brought his people nothing but improvements to their lives. And the fact that you want us to go away makes it obvious that you intend to carry out work here that isn't legal, or of benefit to anyone but yourself.'

'Take my advice and keep quiet, lady,' Anton said. 'You stay in your pathetic little schoolroom where you belong!'

The Chief's face tightened and he barked something angrily to Marundi, who cleared his throat.

'My Chief say, Mr Moolman, you must go now.'

'Go? Is he letting these idiot do-gooders bend his ear? We have a deal and he has to stick to it!'

'My Chief say he will speak again to you. In four days.'

Anton glared and seemed about to launch into another diatribe but thought better of it.

'Goodnight, then. I'll see you again, my friend.'

He turned on his heel and walked quickly away, ignoring Mike and the others.

Marundi grinned.

'My Chief say, please, everyone must stay to drink beer with him, Mr Mike,' he said.

Katie smiled to herself. Luckily she'd brought her camera and could record the expressions of Marion and Fran as they politely tackled the home-brewed beer, which Mike had once described as a mixture of dishwater and some sort of alcoholic back rub!

★ ★ ★

An hour later, when the six of them were able to take their leave of the Chief and make their way down the hill across to the old farmhouse, it was pitch dark with only the starlight to guide them between the stones.

'Well done, everyone,' Mike said. 'I reckon we all went beyond the call of duty tonight!'

'I've tasted worse,' Charles said. 'But I've never felt obliged to drink quite so much of the stuff.'

'I hope nobody noticed that I

'accidentally' knocked over my mug!' Marion said. 'One sip was quite enough for me.'

'What's it made of?' Katie asked. 'It was so sour and didn't taste in the least like any beer I know.'

'It's a mixture of corn and sorghum, boiled up with malt,' Charles said. 'It ferments for days. Everyone who makes beer has a family recipe handed down through the generations and they brew it up for every celebration.'

'Definitely an acquired taste,' Ryan said. 'It's pretty powerful stuff, isn't it?'

'You're right there. I've heard that when the corn finally sinks to the bottom they throw it out to the chickens, who start dancing the tango after just a few pecks at the stuff!' Charles said. 'I'll be glad to get to bed tonight — I can't think why!'

'Just don't start dancing the tango before we reach home,' Marion warned with a smile.

'Everyone is safe to walk, but do not dance, please. Too many rocks.' Marundi's voice came unexpectedly out of the velvety darkness behind them.

'Hi, Marundi, I didn't know you were with us.' Katie felt uncomfortable, hoping he hadn't heard their remarks about the beer. If he had, he didn't say anything.

'I just walk you to your home, keep you on the path. My Chief, he not happy with Mr Moolman,' Marundi said. 'Mr Moolman does not respect him and he does not respect you. He talk very bad to Miss Marion. Is not nice man.'

'Well, I'm hoping to have some good news for the Chief and all your people very soon,' Mike said. 'Then he won't have to deal with Mr Moolman any more.'

He sounds awfully confident, Katie thought. I hope he's right. What if this cousin of Alysha's never arrives?

As they reached the house, the telephone was ringing loudly. Katie hurried inside to answer but it stopped before she could pick up.

'It's after nine,' she said. 'I wonder who that was?'

'They'll call again if it's important,' Fran said. 'Let's have supper. Poor Zukisa must have wondered what's happened to us.'

Discussion

Over a big plate of potatoes, home-grown spinach and spicy chicken stew, they went over the scene with Anton Moolman.

'Did you notice that when you mentioned strip-mining, he didn't deny it?' Ryan asked.

'Because he knows the Chief hasn't a clue what it's all about,' Fran said. 'Maybe we should find some photos on the internet of strip-mines and print them out for him to see. Just giant wastelands of gravel with nothing growing anywhere for miles around.'

'He knows he's in the wrong,' Marion said. 'But did he really think we'd just pack up and go without a fight?'

'I can see the Chief has a soft spot for you, Marion,' Charles joked. 'The minute Moolman talked back at you he got very angry.'

'An old African custom, Charlie, as

you very well know,' Marion said tartly. 'Being polite to old women is part of their upbringing. One of the many good things about a traditional African childhood.'

'Old women? I'll remember you said that, next time you start an argument with me!' Charles grinned.

'Old as in not young,' Marion corrected. 'Old is a state of mind and mine hovers around youthfully middle-aged!'

But there was no doubt that after her operation, she was looking her years, Katie thought. She really needs a break back home in England. Marion was still teaching every morning but relied more and more on Katie and Fran, dividing the class into smaller groups and allowing the girls to handle the reading and writing of the younger ones.

★   ★   ★

Katie allowed the supper conversation to wash over her as she let her thoughts drift.

Without discussing it with Fran or anyone else, she had made the decision to return home to Scotland. The advertising shots she had taken which featured Alysha had long ago been e-mailed to London for the advertising campaign. Alysha now smiled down from billboards all over the country, standing on a wide expanse of stony veldt and holding an appealing little goat, with some huts in the distance.

The same photo appeared on the front of the latest Help At Hand pamphlets and they'd received a few copies by post. She knew Mike had one propped on his bedside table.

She also had literally hundreds of photographs, more than enough for a coffee-table book of the work the charity was doing, and there really was no good reason for her to stay any longer at Kliprand.

She'd had a wonderful, unforgettable experience here but suddenly she was dreadfully homesick and the rolling green hills of Strathcorn were calling her loud and clear. She longed for coolness and soft rain and the gentle burr of the locals chatting to her. She wanted to take wedding pictures again and be involved in the lives of people she'd known all her life. And she wanted to be with Connor.

Alysha was arriving soon but would probably only stay a week or two, so perhaps they could travel back together. As she sat half-listening to the others, she counted the days and realised Connor hadn't e-mailed her for nearly a fortnight.

He'd made no mention of his plans to go back to Strathcorn, although when he'd left for New York, he'd said his stay there would be for six months but could stretch to a year. Every time he wrote he seemed to be having such a great time that he'd probably do his best to stay longer. Or even for ever. She couldn't bear to think of it.

Katie wrenched herself back to the present to hear Charles say that Emily and Marcus would be driving back from Cape Town in the morning.

'I'll be interested in what Marcus has to say about Moolman's mining scheme,' Charles said.

'He'll be furious,' Mike said confidently. 'He knows these people better than we do. He'll know that mining's not the right thing for their lands.'

News

'A copper mine? Great idea,' Marcus said, beaming. It was after lunch the following day and everyone was sitting on the *stoep* enjoying a cold beer to welcome Emily and Marcus back from Cape Town.

'If it's done right, that is,' he continued. 'Not strip-mining, of course, that is entirely destructive. But the Namika have thousands of acres in their name and they don't use even a quarter of it — it's practically desert up in the northern part. They wouldn't be able to keep a single goat alive up there.'

Mike was stunned at Marcus's reaction.

'But a mine of any sort? I can't believe I'm hearing you right! Think what a mine would do to this area.'

'Look, a small mine doesn't have to take up more than a few acres of land.

The Namika wouldn't even be aware of the work if they situated it far from their village. And they could do very well out of it on a profit-sharing basis, which is how these mining companies operate these days. But, hang on, is anyone certain there's copper under their ground anyway? No-one's done any mineral surveys, have they?'

'Not officially. But we're pretty sure Anton Moolman must have taken samples and sent them off to be looked at,' Mike said. 'There's no way he'd go to all this trouble if he wasn't sure.'

'And Alysha's cousin in the government is coming down here?'

'We think so. Nothing's certain. But if the Chief signs up with Moolman that will be disastrous for the whole tribe.'

'We'll just have to think positively,' Emily said comfortably from the depths of her cane chair. 'Marcus, tell them your good news. Oh, but before he does, I must tell you mine! Or rather, all of ours. Just look at this!' She rummaged in her capacious handbag and handed Fran a piece of paper.

'Wow!' Fran grinned in amazement. 'Another order from Phyllis Greenway. This is stunning! Just how big is her interior design business?'

'The shop itself didn't look very big, just terribly smart. But she has a branch in Johannesburg as well, and another in Durban, and apparently she has contracts with game lodges all over the country. And she says these have just the right primitive African look she's wanting.'

'But can we actually make two hundred rugs, d'you think?'

'If Charles would be so kind as to make some more frames, and we invite a lot more women to join the group, I'm sure we can. I brought back as many fabric off-cuts as I could pack into the back of the Jeep, so that should keep us going for several weeks. Wonderful news, isn't it? Now, go on, Marcus, tell them yours!'

Donation

'Well, it turned out that award wasn't just a bit of tin on a piece of ribbon,' Marcus said. 'They gave me a very nice cheque, too. And then they showed the whole lot of nonsense on TV and the next thing, some fellow phones up and asks to meet me. Peter Williams. Turns out he's a retired plastic surgeon who knew my father very well. In fact, he reckons he met me when I was a little nipper but I don't remember him at all.'

'Go on, Marcus, tell them the best bit!' Emily urged. And, unable to stop her excitement bubbling over, she went on. 'Peter gave Marcus a huge donation! Huge!'

'Yep. Enough to build the little obstetrics clinic that I've been dreaming of,' Marcus said. 'This chap made a lot of money in his lifetime but he has no heirs to inherit his estate. And he's getting on in years and had started to think about leaving it all to charity. But, long ago, he drove up through this area on his way to the Augrabies Falls so he knows how badly we need everything, and when he saw the award ceremony on TV he said he knew just what to do with his money!'

'Oh, Marcus, that's wonderful,' Katie said. 'You must be thrilled! If anyone deserves it, you do.'

'And his donation was marvellous but, even better, he says he's going to set up a trust once it's built, so we'll have basic monthly running expenses,' Emily said.

'It sounds almost too good to be true,' Marion said doubtfully. 'I mean, I know you have a pretty face, Marcus, but why should Peter Williams choose to give it all to you?'

'It was really a lucky combination of being in the right place at the right time, and him remembering my father,' Marcus said. 'And when I spoke to him about the clinic I wanted to build, I suggested that the Peter Williams Maternity Clinic had a nice ring to it! He was over the moon. Just the right sort of monument for a doctor, he thought.'

'So did he write you a big cheque, just like that?'

'No, it's all legal and signed and sealed. I went with him to his lawyer to set it all in motion and he told me he's been trying to get the old boy to write another will for ages, ever since his wife died twenty years ago.'

'So how will you go about it?' Mike asked. 'What's the first thing you'll do?'

'Well, I know of an existing farm-house on the other side of Brandveld,' Marcus said. 'It's been standing empty for some time. If I could get the use of that I could convert it into a sort of cottage hospital, with a proper theatre and a well-equipped nursery, and turn some of the bedrooms into wards. And I'd need to organise some sort of transport for expectant mums from round about.'

'And we'll need to hire another doctor to help you,' Emily said firmly. 'And find some qualified nurses for the babies.'

'Lots of planning to do,' Marcus said comfortably. 'All in good time. I'll have to speak to the government chaps at the Department of Health to fund more staff for this, once it's built.'

Ryan turned to his mother.

'Mum, this is really great. I'm delighted you've both got what you wanted. A huge order for the weaving group and a cottage hospital for Marcus. You guys must be very happy.'

'We are!' Emily's face crinkled into a joyful smile. 'And just think, if Marcus hadn't gone down to Cape Town to collect his award, none of this would have happened.'

'All thanks to your mum's nagging, then, Ryan,' Marcus said, squeezing Emily's hand. 'She's a great little nagger. Right, well, I can't sit about gossiping all afternoon. I'll unpack the Jeep, you sit and talk to your son, Em.'

The others drifted away and Ryan sat back and looked teasingly at his mother.

'OK, Mum, I heard the 'we' a couple of times there. So what's the story?'

'Story? Whatever do you mean, Tigs?' But her flush gave her away. 'Actually, Marcus and I were discussing this and we thought it might be a good idea if he came over and stayed with me at Brandveld. Just as a lodger, of course. I have so many spare rooms there. If he's going to be turning that old place into a little hospital he'll need to live somewhere a lot closer than Sandrift. Just for a while.'

'You're absolutely right. I think he's a really good guy and the two of you get on so well. You'll make an excellent team. Go for it!' He leaned over and gave her a hug. 'And who knows how it might work out in the future?'

'Go on with you!' But she looked very pleased. 'I'm very glad you like him, Tigs. That means a lot to me. I like him, too.'

Katie switched on the computer, hoping for an e-mail from Connor. The night before she'd written to him telling him of her decision to return home and she expected a reply. She hoped he'd tell her that he was about to do the same.

The six months he was supposed to spend in New York had passed and unless there was something — or someone — keeping him there, he should be packing up and flying home in a week or two himself.

It's going to take a lot to get on the same page with him again, she thought ruefully. His life's been full of the buzz of a huge city, working with exciting people, going to jazz clubs, spending his weekends sailing and heaven knows what else.

And I've been here in the desert working with children and helping the weavers and taking photographs of goats! I wonder if we'll ever get together properly or if we'll find we've just drifted apart?

She swallowed hard. If only she could see Connor right now, throw her arms around him and be back where they had been before they both left Strathcorn.

Disappointment

She clicked on her e-mail page but the only message waiting for her was one which said *Unable to deliver. Address unknown.*

With a hollow feeling she realised it was the e-mail she'd written to Connor last night. What could this mean? Had he left the company he was working for and joined another, without mentioning it to her? Had he already gone back to Strathcorn? But surely he would have said something, even though his e-mails had been so brief and infrequent lately.

Katie stared at the screen in dismay and a horrible idea popped into her head. Maybe he'd been offered a job by the father of that girl he'd mentioned who took him sailing — Andrea, wasn't she? Mega rich, a yachting champion and probably mad about Connor. Daddy would do anything for her, even find him a job with one of his companies. No wonder he hadn't told her he was leaving!

Huge tears welled up and rolled down Katie's cheeks, blurring the words in front of her.

'Hey, Katie, whatever's wrong?' Fran appeared at the doorway and crossed hurriedly over to her. 'Have you had bad news from home?' She put her arms around Katie, hugging her. 'What is it?'

'It's Connor.' Katie hiccupped. 'He's gone. He's left his job in New York without telling me and my e-mail was returned and I don't know where he is. He might be working for that super-rich man with a yacht who's got a glamorous daughter!'

Even as the words poured out of her, she realised it sounded a bit ridiculous and started to laugh shakily despite her tears.

'Was he ever offered a job by this man?' Fran asked seriously.

'Not as far as I know. OK, I know I'm being silly, Fran. That was a crazy idea. It's just that I miss him and I hate not knowing what's happened.'

'It might be that nothing's happened at all. Don't you have a personal e-mail address to try for him?'

'No — he cancelled it just before he went away.'

'Oh. Well, it could easily be some glitch on the internet,' Fran said. 'Try sending it again and it will probably go through this time. No point in worrying for nothing!'

'You're right, as usual.' Katie sniffed. 'I'll do that.'

She copied out her e-mail quickly and re-sent it.

'Well, leave that for the moment,' Fran said. 'I'm sure it will go through this time. And I came to tell you that Mike's back with Alysha and they both look as if they have something to tell us. But they won't say anything until you're there, too.'

As they left the room, the computer pinged with another e-mail.

Unable to deliver. Address unknown.

'Congratulations!'

'We're going to be married, girlfriend! Mike's proposed and I've accepted!' Alysha sprang up from the chair and joyfully embraced Katie. 'So what do you think of that?'

'Oh, Al, I think that's wonderful! And Mike, congratulations!'

There was a stream of congratulations from everyone around, kisses and handshakes and beams of approval.

'I just wonder what took this man so long!' Alysha ruffled his hair and gave him a quick kiss. 'I was worried I might have to be the one to do the asking!'

Mike was grinning from ear to ear, his eyes never leaving Alysha who looked as though she had just stepped off the front cover of a glossy magazine. She was wearing an elegant green patterned dress, and her hair was pulled into a bun on the top of her head, with loose curls flowing down her back.

Alysha gurgled with happiness.

'Give me a minute. I'll just go and unpack.'

'Don't hurry on my behalf, girlie,' Charles said comfortably. 'You're a sight for sore eyes in that fancy dress!'

'Cheeky man!' Alysha winked at him and disappeared into the house with a small suitcase.

'Well, then, Mike,' Charles said. 'Going to be married, eh? That was fast work.'

'Not really,' Mike said. 'We've been writing to each other for several months.' He couldn't stop smiling and Katie marvelled at how happiness changed his rather stern appearance.

'I'm so glad, Mike,' she said quietly. 'You two are so different but you're perfect for each other, in a funny sort of way. Have you decided when you'll be married? And where?'

'Soon, I hope. And we thought, why not here at Kliprand where all our friends are? Alysha just has to tell her folks back in London and ask them to come out here for the wedding.'

Katie tried to picture a wedding taking place in these surroundings. All her wedding photography back in Strathcorn had featured backgrounds of lush green trees, old stone churches and rolling green lawns. These pictures would certainly be very different!

Then she realised she probably wouldn't be here for her friend's wedding.

She planned to leave South Africa in a week or two and surely arranging a wedding would take a good deal longer than that?

But I won't spoil Alysha's happiness by throwing that spanner in the works, Katie thought. I'm sure they can find a good photographer in Upington for the occasion, and she'll just have to send me some pictures afterwards.

And if she was honest with herself, Katie had to admit that it would be very hard to watch Mike and Alysha getting married while she and Connor were no longer a couple. Because that was the only explanation for the dwindling number of e-mails from him, and now his disappearance.

They'd never been officially engaged. And Connor simply didn't love her any more.

Plans

'So, did you manage to reach your cousin Bona and tell him about this strip mining scheme of Anton Moolman's?' Katie asked Alysha.

It was the morning after Alysha had arrived back at Kliprand, and she had insisted on the three girls taking an early-morning walk down to the stream while it was still cool.

'Sure! I wrote to him as soon as Mike told me about it. And Bona says he'll investigate the title deeds of this land and see what's what. He's arriving tomorrow and I'm dying to meet him.'

'Do you think he'll be able to help?' Fran asked. 'I mean, you told Mike he was a big-wig in the electricity department, didn't you? That's nothing to do with mining.'

'I got it wrong! When I e-mailed him about this mining scheme, he wrote back with an official government e-mail address, and it turned out that he's in the Department of Minerals and Energy. So he'll definitely be able to do something.'

'What incredible timing,' Fran said. 'That dreadful Moolman man is pestering the Chief to sign but Mike begged him not to, so he gave Mike a week to come up with a better idea. And the week ends tomorrow!'

'We Mabendas are known for being in the right place at the right time,' Alysha said smugly. 'Do you know, I just dreamed about this muddy little stream all the time I was away.' She was sitting on a rock and dangling her feet in the slowly moving brown water. 'I kept boasting that everything in Africa was bigger and better! It's odd how strongly connected to Africa I felt once I'd left here.'

'I guess Mike helped with the connection, didn't he?' Katie grinned. 'I'm so pleased that you two have got together by long distance. Mike's a changed man. He says you're planning to marry right here at Kliprand?'

Although she'd mentioned it to Fran, she didn't want to tell Alysha about her own intention to leave very soon. Knowing Alysha, her wedding would take months to organise and Katie just wanted to get home as soon as she could.

'That's right! We both want a real African wedding. Something that will make us feel part of this place for ever.'

'So — no church and no long white dress for you, then?' Katie teased. 'Bush boots and khaki shorts, right?'

'Silly! I haven't thought that far yet. But I e-mailed my folks first thing this morning and asked them to fly over as soon as they can. And no church; we're not church people.'

'So no minister, then?'

'Mike spoke to Emily, and she knows a lovely minister of the Free Unitarian church who's prepared to perform the ceremony out here in the veldt. Although we have to go down to Cape

Town to do a civil ceremony, as well, in front of a magistrate, to make it official. Apparently the law here says marriages can only take place under a fixed roof!'

Right Idea

'Al, have you talked about what you'll do after you're married? I mean, Mike's committed to working here — are you going to give up your modelling?' Katie was serious for a moment. 'I honestly can't imagine you living in the bush for ever.'

'Neither can I. I mean, I'll gladly help run the weaving, but I don't see why I shouldn't do a few modelling jobs in Europe. We'll see how it works out.'

'Mike could work anywhere, if he wanted to,' Fran said. 'He's been out in Africa for ten years but he could easily find employment back in Australia. And once you two start a family . . . '

'Hold on there!' Alysha laughed. 'Forward planning is good, girl, but that's going a bit far down the line. Still, Australia is wonderful, and I'd be up for living anywhere just as long as it's with Mike.'

She's got the right idea, Katie thought, suddenly miserable. If only I'd agreed to go with Connor to New York, we'd still be together — maybe even married by now. It's all my fault for agreeing to live separate lives. I must have been mad.

'Let's go back and find some breakfast,' she said, standing up. 'I'm starving and I know Zukisa's corn bread will be out of the oven by now.'

★ ★ ★

When Bona Mabenda arrived at Kliprand the following morning, he came in a long, black saloon with tinted windows, driven by a uniformed chauffeur.

'Wow,' Mike muttered. 'This looks like a serious government delegation.'

He and Alysha stepped forward to greet the rotund little man who alighted from the back seat of the car and limped over to the waiting group.

'My cousin Alysha? I greet you!' He took Alysha's hand in two of his own and bowed. 'I am Bona Mabenda.'

'Hello, Bona,' Alysha said. She towered above him and bent to kiss his cheek. 'I can't believe we're meeting at last. I'd given up all hope of finding any of my family here in South Africa, and here you are!'

'And here I am!' Bona said. 'Under-assistant Secretary to the Office of the Minister of Minerals and Energy, at your service.' He looked around the assembled company through his rimless spectacles, beaming. 'Am I in time for tea?' he asked.

'Of course,' Marion said. 'It's always time for tea!'

Bona looked at her hopefully.

'You're from England?' he asked. 'Do you by any chance drink Earl Grey?'

Bona's Help

By the time he'd finished three cups of tea and several ginger biscuits Zukisa had baked in his honour, the full story of Anton Moolman's plans for an open-cast mine had been explained and Bona made it clear that he would deal with him.

'If Mr Moolman wants to mine for copper, he has clearly surveyed the land in some way and is aware of the possibilities,' he said. 'But I will send a team of government surveyors down to double check. If they decide it's economically viable, there are several mining houses who would jump at the chance to develop a mine, strictly on a profit-sharing basis with my people here.'

'That's what we were hoping you'd say,' Mike said. 'And we're also hoping that when Anton Moolman comes over this afternoon to ask the Chief to sign away his mineral rights, you could sit in on that meeting?'

'Just try to stop me!' Bona said. 'But before we meet him, could you show me the good work you've been doing here? I believe you have actually laid on water for the people of the village?'

Mike, Charles and Ryan gave their visitor a guided tour of Kliprand, showing him the wells they'd drilled, the school and the weaving workshop. He asked intelligent questions about everything and was particularly interested in Ryan's work as a vet.

'I remember when I was a boy here, my father's cows suffered some terrible affliction. His herd became very small and there was nothing he could do.'

'That sounds like brucellosis,' Ryan said. 'It used to be pretty common all over, especially in Africa. It's very contagious. But don't worry, I've injected every cow on Kliprand against it, as well as East Coast fever.'

'Mike, I can see that all of you at

Help At Hand have made a very big difference to my people,' Bona said. 'And I think my little cousin has found a good man to share her life.'

Mike smiled at his description of the six-foot-tall Alysha being little.

'Then I hope you'll put in a good word for me with her parents. They're coming over here soon and they've not met me.'

'You can depend on it, my friend,' Bona said.

Puzzled

After lunch, Bona asked to be taken across to pay his respects to the Chief.

'He and I must meet before Mr Moolman arrives, to discuss matters,' he said. 'It will be a real joy for me to meet my Chief after these many years.'

He went to his room and returned with a bottle of expensive whisky and a gift-wrapped box of glasses.

'Always an acceptable gift,' he said cheerfully. 'And I came prepared because I've never acquired the taste for the beer he is sure to offer me, I'm afraid. I've been away from my roots for too long.'

'He's a sweetie,' Fran said, watching Bona walk across to the huts with Zukisa leading the way. 'I'm sure he's going to send Moolman off with an official flea in his ear.'

Mike took Alysha's hand.

'Come on, I want to show you our corn from Australia. We've just planted a tiny patch but it seems to be flourishing.'

Katie watched them go, Mike's arm around Alysha's shoulders in an easy embrace. Lucky Alysha, to have found her own true love in such an unexpected place.

The half-acre of green shoots that had sprung up in the past fortnight was Mike's pride and joy, the whole reason he'd come to Kliprand. If this experiment with the hybrid seed was successful, the Namika could be self-sufficient in a year or two, now that they had water for crops.

Homesickness

So perhaps Fran was right when she said that Mike might be wanting to move on soon, once this corn was established. He and Alysha could settle anywhere. Or maybe they'd never settle, but move from one aid project to another all over the world.

Katie grimaced at the thought. She couldn't wait to go back home to Scotland and stay there for a long time. Home seemed increasingly attractive.

Just then, the telephone rang and she went into the house to answer it, but there was only a loud humming on the line.

She hung up, puzzled. This was the third time this had happened lately, but Mike had said the telephone company had checked the line and it wasn't down anywhere.

Katie wandered back to the *stoep*

and spent some time looking at the latest shots on her digital camera.

★ ★ ★

In the middle of the afternoon a fast-moving column of dust heralded the arrival of Anton Moolman at the village, and the villagers could be seen slowly making their way towards the hut of the Chief, crowding together outside to watch the proceedings.

Mike watched, anxious.

'I wish I knew what was going on there.'

Suddenly a young man broke away from the group and came trotting down the hill and up the path to the farmhouse.

'The Chief is saying, please all to come.'

'Well, we can't refuse an official invitation!' Charles grinned and everyone headed across.

The congregated villagers parted silently to let them through into the darkened interior of the hut, where Bona sat on an upturned crate next to the Chief and Anton Moolman sat on a plastic chair opposite, looking impatient. Marundi stood behind, waiting to translate.

Between them sat a set of garishly coloured glass bowls and the contract which Anton had left for the Chief to sign.

'Don't know why you people have to be sticking your noses into this,' Anton grumbled. 'I've just been explaining to Mr Mabenda here that this business is between the Chief and me.'

'On the contrary, Mr Moolman, you have no business here with anyone. Not my Chief and not the Namika people.' Bona rose from his crate and stood over Anton, suddenly authoritative in his three-piece suit and shining black shoes. 'I have done some research on the original title deeds to this land, which was given by the government to my tribe in nineteen fifty-one.' He unfolded a thick document, yellowed with age. 'Fortunately, I found these in the office of the Surveyor General.'

'You have title deeds to this waste-land?' Anton asked in disbelief.

'Luckily, yes. Because we, the Namika people, were removed from our original tribal lands when diamonds were discovered on them, the government of the day tried to make things sound better by giving us all rights to all minerals found below the surface of the earth here. Of course, they didn't expect that there'd be any.'

'Wasn't that pretty unusual?' Ryan asked. 'I thought mineral rights here were separate from the ownership of the land?'

'Yes, that's why these title deeds are exceptional,' Bona said. 'I have a feeling that one of the missionaries who were working amongst the tribe at the time might have had a hand in drafting these.'

'And it means that now copper has been discovered, the Namika are entitled to decide how to mine the copper and who will do it,' Mike said triumphantly. 'And with Bona to advise them, they'll be sure to get the best deal from one of the recognised mining groups. The ones that build hospitals and proper schools and train the workers and award their children bursaries to study.'

'But I am the one who found the copper here!' Anton snapped. 'If it had been left to these people, they'd have lived on in poverty for ever. And besides, Chief, I can promise you electricity, too, once we get going with the mine. You will see, you'll become a rich man.'

Disgust

The Chief stared at him stonily and muttered something to Marundi behind him.

'My Chief say, better that all our people have work and have a better life,' Marundi said. 'Better we have a good mine that keeps our land for our cattle but gives us also a proper school, proper road, proper shops. He say, you are a foolish man if you think television for one person is better for us.'

And it struck Katie suddenly that the shrewd old Chief had understood a lot of what Anton had been saying all the time, and probably everyone else, as well.

With an explosive expression of disgust, Anton rose to his feet angrily.

'If you think a big mining company will give you more than I will, you're a bigger fool than I thought you were. Wait till your people see how they're going to be cheated and see how they blame you.'

'That's not going to happen, Mr Moolman,' Bona said. 'Our government has laws in place which demand that mining companies now draw up share schemes for all employees, so Namika men who work on the mine, when it comes, will be shareholders.'

Anton's fists bunched ominously but he just glared at Bona.

'And maybe I should inform you that you can expect a visit from the police very soon,' Bona continued. 'Your name has come up in connection with illegal diamond dealings at your farm. I hope you'll be able to explain everything to their satisfaction, because the penalty for dealing in diamonds without a permit is extremely severe, as I am sure you know.'

Everyone watched as Anton stormed out of the hut and drove off at full speed.

'I think that went very well!' Bona said cheerfully. 'Mr Moolman won't trouble us again. In fact, I don't think you'll see him for a long time once the police have spoken with him.'

Marundi beamed and signalled the women outside the huts.

'My Chief has brewed beer especially for this day. You are all his honoured guests for this occasion.'

'Er — we'll say goodbye here, I think,' Mike said regretfully, edging towards the door. 'We have — um — work to do. But I'm delighted everything seems to be working out well. And I know Bona will want to stay and celebrate, won't you, Bona?'

'Certainly, it is an honour to drink with my Chief,' Bona said politely. He didn't sound happy.

But the noise of the party went on long into the darkness and at some point Bona must have rediscovered his roots because when he left the following morning, he carried with him a big bottle of the home-brewed beer he'd been enjoying.

Odd Behaviour

The following morning, just as Katie and Fran were walking across to the schoolroom laden with the children's work books, the phone rang.

'I'll get it,' Fran said. 'You go over, Marion's waiting for these marks.'

When she joined Katie and Marion in the classroom some time later, her cheeks were flushed and she looked oddly excited.

'Who was that?' Katie asked.

'No-one. Well, no-one important. Just someone for Mike. I told him to call back later; Mike's off with Charles admiring his corn seedlings.' She turned to Marion. 'Shall Katie and I take the little ones for reading while you give the older ones their work books?'

That's odd, Katie thought. She's definitely changing the subject.

The lessons passed quickly and

Marion was dismissing the children at the end of the morning just as Alysha and Emily walked past from their session with the weavers, so the four women headed back to the house together.

'Zola has turned into a real star,' Emily said. 'She thinks of such beautiful colour combinations and her weaving is perfect. I'm going to ask her to be in charge of the work room when I'm back at Brandveld. I'll still come over here every week, of course, but I won't be staying here overnight any more.'

'We'll miss you, Emily,' Fran said, hugging her.

'Oh, you'll still see plenty of me. And I'm sure Tigger will bring you over when he comes to visit his old mum. I've noticed he seems to be very fond of your company!' Her eyes twinkled mischievously, but Fran blushed slightly.

'I enjoy his company, too, of course. I mean, he is so interesting to talk to and he's awfully nice . . . '

'Yes, he is.' Emily took Fran's hand in hers. 'I'm very pleased the two of you have become such good friends. I used to worry that Tigs was so wrapped up in his work that he'd never find time to, well, meet the right girl. But now he has.'

Fran's face flamed even redder.

'We're just good friends,' she mumbled.

'Oh, I know that. But I've always said that being good friends is the best sort of start to something more serious, dear!'

Katie winced for Fran. Emily was a dear soul, but even though Katie knew that Fran would like nothing better than to be the right girl for Ryan, she wouldn't enjoy these helpful comments.

Fran suddenly quickened her pace and walked ahead, hurrying up the stairs of the house. Before the others had arrived, she hurried out again, with Ryan in tow.

'Bye,' she said breathlessly. 'Ryan and I have to go to Brandveld to fetch something.'

'Goodness, Tigs, neither of you has had lunch!' Emily protested. 'Can't you go after you've eaten?'

''Fraid not, Mum, there's a delivery of vaccine that's just arrived for me,' Ryan mumbled. 'It can't wait. See you later.'

The two of them drove off in a rush.

'That's so odd,' Marion said. 'I thought he collected a big parcel of vaccine only three days ago. That vet laboratory should really be better organised.'

* * *

Over lunch Katie was silent. She knew she had to tell everyone she planned to leave soon, but once she said it out loud, her departure would become a fact.

I'll tell them tomorrow, she thought, when everyone's here together.

'Katie, the women are going to be dyeing some of the weaving fabric after lunch.' Emily broke into her thoughts.

'They've told me how their grandmothers used to dye fabric purple by boiling it up with some sort of indigenous red seed, and Zola brought a big sack of it she'd collected in the veldt.'

'Purple? I know in Mali they used to collect wild indigo leaves to boil up to make the most wonderful dark blue,' Marion said.

'If they really can produce a purple dye, it would be lovely,' Emily said. 'That's one colour we don't get much from the factory and it blends so well with blue and turquoise strips. I've given them some white pieces to see what they can do. Anyway, they're taking one of those huge pots of theirs down to the river and I wonder if that might make a colourful photograph for your collection?'

'Thanks for the heads-up. I'll go and take a look,' Katie said, although privately she was pretty sure she'd taken far too many shots already. The proposed coffee-table book of her photographs was the one bright spark on the horizon and she knew she'd have to contact the head office of Help At Hand as soon as she returned home.

Before she left the house, a small, unreasonable flicker of hope made her switch on the computer and look at her e-mails, but there was nothing from Connor. She felt angry with herself for even expecting one after all this time, and abruptly disconnected. She picked up her camera bag and strolled down to the river.

Thoughtful

The women were laughing as they paddled about in the warm, muddy stream, their reddish brown skirts hiked up at the waist. They'd boiled a huge pot of water on a makeshift fire on the bank and a great bundle of fabric strips was bubbling away in what appeared to be black water. But as she watched, one of the women lifted out a swathe of wet fabric with a stick and it had turned a pretty mauve with streaks of darker tones.

Katie took some shots, wondering if this would prove to be successful. Emily had tried experimenting with dye from local plants before, but the colours had all dried into pale shades of orange or tan, and the weavers preferred using the brighter fabrics direct from the factory.

I must buy a couple of rugs before I leave, she thought. Mum would love one, and once I get my own flat in

Strathcorn, a rug would make a wonderful souvenir.

She wandered up along the stream, idly picking stems of dried grass as she went.

The afternoon heat was slowly cooling and the small brown birds, which seemed to take a siesta in the middle of the day, were starting to emerge and swoop across the water. Katie sat down under a thorn tree and watched a pair of them sitting on a frond of thick grass, energetically pecking the seeds in unison, chirping and fussing as they ate.

It's odd how almost no African birds really sing, she thought sleepily, they just chatter and tweet. Mum's garden was always filled with birdsong . . . That was the last thought she had as her eyes closed and she drifted off, her head resting on a thick tussock of grass.

When she woke, she became aware of someone sitting nearby. She blinked hard, forcing herself to wake up properly.

It was Connor.

'Hello, sleepyhead,' he said softly.

'You're A Dream'

Katie sat upright and stared.

'You're a dream,' she said flatly.

'Nope, sweetheart. I'm here. Took me four days to reach you, but I made it. Late connections, terrible roads.'

He had an odd, hesitant expression, as if he were waiting for her reaction, but she just looked at him, unable to speak.

'Stunned mullet comes to mind,' he said carefully. 'I was hoping you'd be a little bit pleased to see me.'

'I am, of course I am.' But she couldn't keep the hot tears from welling up and spilling down her cheeks. 'Oh, Connor, why didn't you write to me? It's been three weeks since your last e-mail. I thought you'd just decided to end everything. Us, I mean.'

'Katie!' Connor pulled her to her feet and took her roughly in his arms, holding her so tightly she could hardly breathe. 'End everything? Are you nuts?'

She giggled into his chest, relief flooding though her.

'But why didn't you answer my e-mails?' She broke away to look at him. 'And why have you come? And how did you get here?'

'I'll answer those question backwards. I got here because your very kind friends, Fran and Ryan, picked me up from Brandveld where the coach dropped me.'

Surprise

'So it was you who phoned this morning?'

'Yes, I'd been trying to reach you on the phone for a couple of days but the connection was impossible. Twice I heard your voice but you obviously couldn't hear mine, so I just gave up and decided to phone from Cape Town, once I'd arrived in South Africa.'

'So Fran knew! No wonder she and Ryan acted so mysteriously.'

'I asked her not to tell you. I wanted to be a surprise.'

'You are! The best kind of surprise.' Katie couldn't stop grinning with joy. 'But what made you decide to come all the way over to South Africa?'

'Because I'd just had enough of being without you, I guess. I was fed up with New York and I missed you too much. You seemed to be having such a great time here that I thought I'd come and see for myself.'

She hugged him close.

'OK. Excellent reason. But why didn't you write to me properly? All those quick little notes, as though you didn't have time even to think about me! And why was your e-mail address not working for the past two weeks?'

'I guess because I officially left the office ten days ago and just took a side trip down to the Grand Canyon. I wanted to see a bit of the country before I left.'

'You could have let me know! I was so worried. I pictured all sorts of disasters.' She wasn't going to tell him she'd pictured him in Andrea's arms on her father's yacht.

'Sorry, sweetheart.' He took a deep breath. 'I wasn't too sure what I was going to do and until I knew, I didn't want to write to you. To tell the truth, the past month I went through a patch of feeling very mixed up. About life in general. About where I was heading.'

'Did this mixed-up feeling include what's her name — the girl whose father took you out on his yacht?' Her voice quivered.

'Andrea? Good lord, no! She was a nice girl but she was just one of the gang at the office. No, it was my music. Remember I mentioned playing a few times in a jazz club?'

'Yes. Well, I think you only told me about it once.' If Andrea was out of the picture that she'd foolishly dreamed up, Katie felt she could handle anything.

'I guess I didn't want you to see how keen I was becoming on that side of my life. I started going to the same club almost every night and joining in with a few sets and it was great. They were real professionals.'

'Better than the Laddies Of Loch Muir?' She giggled, remembering the group Connor had played with in the Strathcorn pub.

'On another planet, music-wise. Anyway, they were about to go on the road, and they had gigs lined up right across

412

the States, but their regular sax player let them down at the last minute. So they offered me his job. A twelve-week tour from New York to Los Angeles, and just about every jazz club in between.'

'Oh, Connor, that must have been a dream come true for you! But . . . it looks as though you said no?'

'In the end. But I took ages to make up my mind. Just the thought of travelling around in a van with that great bunch of guys and making music every night . . . it was very appealing.'

'So how could you refuse an offer like that?'

'I admit it was tempting, but I turned it down because I couldn't see you enjoying that kind of life. No roots, driving from town to town every couple of days, not knowing anyone.'

'You're such a lovely man. But why didn't you at least ask me? I might have agreed.'

Although it was difficult to sound indignant when she was so relieved, the thought of driving in a van across

America certainly held no appeal.

'Yes, you might have. But you'd have agreed because you'd have thought I wanted to do it. I know you, Katie, your kind heart would have ruled your head, but you'd probably have hated every minute. Anyway, I could tell from your e-mails that you were ready to go back to Strathcorn and actually, I'm pretty homesick myself.'

'Oh, good! I am, too, dreadfully. In fact I've been planning to go back next week but my timing is terrible because Alysha and Mike are getting married soon and — oh, you haven't met Mike. He's a lovely guy, and — '

'I've met them all, I think. Marion, Charles . . . I had tea with them before I came looking for you. And I heard all about their wedding plans. Apparently Alysha's parents are flying out next week and the two of them want to be married in a fortnight. We could stay for that, couldn't we?'

'We could stay for ever, now that you're here!'

'Wrong, my darling. We have wedding plans of our own, remember?'

★ ★ ★

It was the day of the wedding, and the old farmhouse at Kliprand was buzzing. Everyone in the village was invited to the festivities and it was set to be a celebration to remember.

Connor and Mike had helped Charles and Ryan to knock together several sturdy trestles for the food and they were laying them out in the shade of the pepper tree by the barn.

Katie was trundling back and forth from the house with paper plates and plastic forks to pile on the tables.

'Here's the last of the essentials,' she said, placing some bowls of salt on each trestle. 'I'm off to help Alysha get dressed now. Just wait till you see her outfit — she'll knock your socks off!'

'Alysha's good at that!' Charles laughed. 'I thought her mum and dad were going to be a bit gobsmacked at this whole turn of events, too, but they seem very happy.'

'They're used to her,' Katie said. 'And what's not to like about this man?' She ruffled Mike's hair and hurried off to the room where Alysha was dressing.

Alysha's parents had arrived two days previously and once they'd met Mike, they thoroughly approved of him as a husband for their daughter.

'If you are Alysha's choice, then you are the man for her,' her father said simply, shaking Mike's hand.

He was delighted, too, to make the acquaintance of Bona, the cousin he'd never met.

Bona came down from Pretoria and was ceremoniously installed in the second best hut of the Chief's, with a bed. He seemed to take on the rôle of a senior member of the Namika tribe with enjoyment and the two cousins talked for hours.

Hazel Mabenda took charge of the catering for the party. She was a large, capable woman who made friends with

Zukisa and seemed able to communicate, although she had no words of Namika and Zukisa had very few of English. But Zukisa knew exactly what was required for a Namika feast, and soon the kitchen was full of women from the huts boiling up vast quantities of dried beans and onions, chopping carrots and stirring maize meal porridge.

'I'd always imagined little dainty bits and pieces and a three-tier wedding cake when Al got married!' Hazel said.

'Well, as to the cake, Emily's making a big chocolate one and bringing it over this afternoon,' Marion said. 'And Fran and Ryan went shopping in Upington for a few special things for the bride's table yesterday.'

'Bride's table?' Hazel asked. 'I didn't think we'd have one of those?'

'Of course,' Marion said firmly. 'This party will go on for hours and I don't think we want to stand all the time, do you?'

'Alysha tells me you're thinking of

taking a long break back in England,' Hazel said, looking at the older woman sympathetically. 'You've had a tough life in all these out-of-the-way places, haven't you? You deserve a holiday.'

'Yes, as soon as Mike and Alysha come back from their honeymoon, I thought I'd go home. Enjoy the shops, the hot water on tap, the television programmes . . . '

'But not the weather?'

Marion laughed.

'Believe me, rain will be a treat!'

Unusual Venue

Behind the barn, Charles was keeping an eye on the progress of the main course and wandered over to report back to the temporary carpenters.

'Looks good, and it should be just about right by the time the service is over,' he said. 'Speaking of which, isn't it about time you went and tidied up, Mike? Put on your best bib and tucker?'

'Lots of time,' Mike said comfortably. 'Anyway, it's Alysha everyone will want to look at. I just have to put on a clean shirt!'

'I hope you're joking,' Ryan said. 'Those shorts won't pass Marion's eagle eye!'

The minister had driven over that morning and talked to Mike and Alysha for a while. Reverend Atkins was a tall, good-humoured man who took the unusual venue in his stride.

'I've held marriage services down a mine and on a boat,' he said cheerfully. 'It's not the place that counts, it's the love and commitment between the two of you. Have you written your own vows? Many couples do these days.'

'Heavens, no,' Mike said in alarm. 'We want a proper old-fashioned wedding with all the right words!'

'But not obey,' Alysha said firmly. 'That word's out! But love, cherish, and all that good stuff.'

'I'll be sure to include all the good stuff,' the Reverend said with a twinkle.

★ ★ ★

It was half an hour before the wedding was due to begin and dusk was falling, the endless canopy of blue sky fading to star-sprinkled black velvet.

The tables were laid with enormous dishes of food and big pots of beer had mysteriously appeared from the huts. The long table on the *stoep*, laid with a white cloth, boasted champagne, a chocolate cake and cold salads for those who didn't fancy chunks of beef.

The villagers had gathered in a huge, excited crowd along the riverbank and Fran and Katie were in the bedroom putting the finishing touches to Alysha's outfit while she did her make-up.

'Forget something old and something new,' she said, gazing critically into the mirror. 'I've got something Western and something African!'

She was dressed in a long, stylish orange skirt with lines of darker braid around the bottom, something she'd been told Xhosa women wore. Her dark green turban, the woven fabric from Mali, was twisted with a flourish and fastened with a brooch she'd had made from the green malachite stone which had told them there might be copper at Kliprand. Beaded necklaces that she had borrowed from Emily completed the look.

'I know Mum expected me to be a traditional bride,' she said. 'But I wanted to sort of . . . include my roots.

And show Mike I'll be with him wherever else he goes in Africa! Besides, this turban's pretty cool, isn't it?'

'You look extremely cool,' Fran said. 'Only you could make an outfit like this glamorous, Alysha!'

'Oh, you need something blue . . . and here it is.' Katie produced a lacy blue and white garter. 'Made with my own fair hands.'

'Wicked, girlfriend!' Alysha kissed Katie and hugged her close. 'Now I'm the perfect mix.'

'You are, you know,' Katie whispered, suddenly close to tears. 'You and Mike. Perfect. And this wedding is exactly right for the two of you.'

'Who'd have thought it, eh? Our three weeks in Africa certainly didn't stick to the plan.'

'But it's all worked out far better than our plan! You've met the man you love and I've had an incredible experience. And made friends with people I'll never forget. Especially you,

Fran.' She drew Fran into the circle and the three of them hugged fiercely until Katie broke away and picked up her camera.

'Come on, time to get out there, Mike's waiting.'

Blessings

Alysha slipped on the garter and stepped out on to the *stoep*, pausing to hug her mother who was dabbing away tears. Marion squeezed her hand as she passed and Charles gave her a gruff peck.

'Good luck, girlie,' he whispered. 'My, you look a picture.'

Mr Mabenda solemnly took his daughter's arm and Fran and Katie, joined by Ryan and Connor, followed them down the steps towards the stream where Emily and Marcus were waiting. The tall silhouette of Mike could be seen against the water's edge. Miraculously, he was wearing a suit and had brushed his hair.

And, as they walked along the rocky path towards the minister, the villagers' voices rose in song, their perfect harmonies echoing across the darkening valley. Cowhide drums beat a steady rhythm and women in the crowd started ululating, their high-pitched yodelling sending goosebumps down Katie's spine. She clutched Connor's hand.

'I just can't break the spell and take photos. I'll wait until afterwards.'

Alysha reached Mike's side and they looked into each other's eyes, the love passing between them almost tangible.

'Dearly beloved,' Reverend Atkins said, his voice rising against the sound of the evening breeze which had sprung up. 'We are gathered together in the sight of God . . .'

And at that, the sun began to set, bestowing its golden blessing on the congregation below.

THE END